DELLA'S DIARY

Renee Darcy

Published by: Bright Little Light Press

First Print Edition: 2017

Copyright © 2017 Renee Darcy

ISBN: 1-946804-03-7
ISBN-13: 978-1-946804-03-7

To all the peppers out there:

You're not crazy.

You're just preparing for a future that hasn't happened yet.

Other Titles by Renee Darcy
America's Favorite Couple
A reality TV romance, Book 1

Coming Summer 2017
A reality TV romance, Book 2

FORWARD

I started writing this novel in 2014. I got about halfway through it, paused, and picked it up again in late 2015. Once I finished it, it sat around on my hard drive, collecting metaphorical digital dust.

It wasn't until early 2017 that I re-read *Della's Diary* in prep for editing it and preparing it for publication.

Some of the things that I wrote in this novel in 2014 have proven to be surprisingly prescient.

In light of some of the things that have been happening since the presidential election in early 2017, it may seem that parts of this book are overly political, or that they were written in direct response to current events. I assure you, that's all entirely unintentional. In editing *Della's Diary*, I had to make a decision about whether or not to leave it in, now that certain things are playing out on the global and national stage.

In the end, I asked myself: "What would Della do?"

The answer was pretty clear. Della would want these things to remain in the book. She'd want you all to think about these things, and pay attention to what's happening in the world - and do your best to be prepared. So, to honor Della, I've left it alone.

Don't worry, though - if it ever feels like too much doom and gloom, just keep going. In life, and in this book. Della's plucky spirit always shines through in the end, and yours can, too, if you let it.

November 2014

Saturday, November 1, 2014

Starting a new journal. I've found that so many days pass without me really knowing what I did that day. And as Ben grows up, I want to capture... everything. It seems like every week or month he's doing something new, and he's not the little guy he was even last year. I want to remember all of this as he grows.

Plus, it would be nice to have some notes on my achievements, trials and tribulations to look back on. I think it'll help put whatever I'm going through at a given moment into perspective, to be able to look back on old diary journals.

And then there's the fact that writing all this stuff down helps me process things. Sometimes I don't even realize what's going on in my brain until I start typing, and then things just come out and suddenly I'm like "Whoa! That's where that came from!"

So yeah. Here I am. Let's see...

Obviously the date is up there at the top of the page. As of the beginning of this journal, I'm still a freelance writer. My clients are happy with me, and my income is enough to help with some of the 'extra' expenses, like Ben's karate, the second car payment and saving for his college. But Jim's job still pays most of our bills, so I feel kind of like my career comes second.

My main job is being a mother to Ben. My second job is making sure our household runs smoothly so Jim can relax when he gets home. Since he's the primary earner, I feel like it's my job to do all the cooking and cleaning and bill paying and car maintenance and... everything. So I guess my career comes third?

Wow, that's depressing. See, revelations already! I don't think I've ever really said that to myself before.

Well, anyway - on to the actual events of my life.

Hubby's birthday was yesterday, and I turned myself into a virtual slave to give him a nice day and a good dinner even though we're broke right now. When Jim's car broke down last week, the repairs really wiped us out. But he works so hard for me and Ben, I feel like I have to do what I can to make life nice for him - I don't want him to feel how tight our finances are right now on a special occasion like his birthday. I do what I can.

Thank God Ben was able to go Trick-or-Treating with friends yesterday, and I didn't have to try to fit in *that*, too. But all this everything means I'm exhausted today, and all I want to do is relax - but we've got stuff going on all weekend.

Today, Ben has a karate meet, and I promised some of the other moms that I'd help with refreshments after. Of course, Barbara is one of those moms - I just know she'll find something to complain about. Bah. Why is she always so holier-than-thou about - well, about everything?

Anyway, on top of today, we're getting together tomorrow with the usual crew for a birthday party for hubby. I was thinking I might make pumpkin bread for that get-together.

I wish we weren't broke this year, and I could have just bought him something.

LATER

Ben did really well at his karate meet! I was so proud of him. One of the other moms was a little snotty about my chocolate chip cookies (Barb!) - I did the recipe that has the nuts, not the recipe that has the Jacques Torres chocolate chips - but I didn't really have time for anything else with Jim's birthday yesterday. They hold up well, anyway. What's so wrong with giving the kids a little bit of sugar after they've had all that exercise? It won't hurt them! Just because I didn't make some sort of organic veggie snack that half the kids probably wouldn't have wanted to touch anyway is no excuse for her to turn her nose up at me.

And while I'm on the topic, I may be a little bit rounder than some of the other moms, and so what if I don't dye my hair and you can see some gray? I challenge any of those other moms to hold down a sedentary freelance job - being their own bosses and not getting paid time off or insurance or a retirement account or any of life's other little luxuries - and still keep their figure trim while being a good parent and juggling all of my household and family stuff. Hah!

Must remember to make some oatmeal cookies the next time I'm on refreshments - just to spite her.

Sunday, November 2, 2014

Birthday party for Jim today. We got together with friends and spent the day cooking him some of his favorite foods and playing board games. He's always enjoyed that. We did spend more on food for everyone than I wanted to spend, with us being so broke right now - but that's what credit cards are for, right? At least we cooked - it's still cheaper than feeding everyone at a restaurant.

Of course we got a late start. I had a major headache this morning, and then Jim was stuck in the bathroom forever, and then Ben's sitter was late, and I wanted to stop at Starbucks for something sugary and caffeinated before I had to face the crew - so we got there a half hour late. To his own birthday party!

Yes, I was embarrassed. You'd think after all these years with Jim and his meandering and his taking forever to get out the door, I'd be ok with being late to things. But I've just never been able to shake that whole "Be on time or it's a sign of disrespect" thing from my upbringing. Being a mom has given me a whole new perspective on time… but I still can't be ok with being late.

Fortunately, even though we were late, they had just barely begun cooking. And here I thought they would have already done the cooking ahead of time, so we could get right to the board games. We didn't even get to start gaming until around three o-clock, and we were supposed to leave by eight to relieve the sitter. Jim chose Caverna - it's sort of like Agricola, but set in caves - but of course with this crew, games always take longer than they're supposed to take to play. Even with me chivvying them along, I finally had to drag Jim away around nine, and the game still wasn't over! I felt bad making him leave the party before the game had even finished, but we'd already run late on the sitter and I know Ben can be fussy about bedtime if we're not there to put him down.

Still, I think Jim had a good day, so I guess that's all that matters. I just wish we could have timed things a little better to fit everything in properly.

Monday, November 3, 2014

Monday, again. Since summer's over and school is back in session, Monday has become my favorite day of the week. Don't get me wrong, I love spending time with my husband and son on the weekend - but it's impossible for me to get anything done when they're underfoot. And relaxing? Hah. No such thing.

Monday is me time. Monday is the day when I get to get some house cleaning done, and some work, and I may even put my heels up for an hour or two and stare mindlessly at the TV. Ben's at school, Jim's at the office, and the day stretches unsullied before me, a tabula rasa for me to accomplish *my* objectives. Well, and satisfy my clients. Super Mom and Working Wife is never really off duty.

LATER

I was poking around Netflix for something to watch while I ate my lunch, and I came across this reality TV show about people preparing for various types of disaster scenarios. At first, I was thinking it was going to be another one of those horrific guilty pleasure reality shows - they'd somehow be making fun of a bunch of idiots who are wasting their time preparing for ever-more-unlikely scenarios to bring about the End of the World as We Know It. I turned it on, making bets with myself about whether I'd even be able to sit through a single episode.

I was surprised. The show was a production by that company that also makes the awesome travel magazines, and it actually seemed to be trying to take these people seriously. The producers actually included subtitles on the screen that provided additional details whenever someone on the show brought up unusual ideas, and they kept giving a breakdown of the odds that whatever disaster would actually occur (ranging from highly unlikely to ain't gonna happen). But the thing that struck me was that the people on the show, for the most part, actually didn't seem to be the crazy conspiracy theorists I was expecting. They seemed like reasonable people, taking reasonable steps to protect their families in the face of some sort of disaster that they perceived as a legitimate threat to their family.

In other words, I could actually relate to some of the people on the show. I might not agree with their crazy ideas about threats, but I could see some sense in having some food and water on hand in the event of a disaster.

Take Superstorm Sandy, for example. It knocked out power to a lot of homes on the East Coast - in some cases for a while. I think it hit New Jersey pretty bad, too - took out a lot of houses. And then there was Hurricane Irene - that washed out roads in Vermont, and left some towns stranded for nearly a week before help could get to them. They're still rebuilding stretches of Route 2 out in Western Massachusetts.

Granted, Boston isn't likely to get stranded, but we have had power outages - and I could see some disasters impacting us here. Flooding is an issue sometimes. Billerica had some bad floods a few years ago and actually got declared a disaster area. A bunch of people lost power, and had major damage to their homes. And then there was that freak tornado in Revere recently. I don't think about it often, but I guess unexpected stuff happens even around here.

Maybe I should talk to Jim about keeping a few food and water supplies on hand in the event of a legitimate emergency or disaster.

Tuesday, November 4, 2014

Today is election day. It's a mid-term election, which means no president - but control of the Senate is precarious just now. The House is already in the hands of the Republicans, and only five Democratic seats stand between the Republican party and control of the Senate. I'm not sure how much I care, really, because they're all so much talk and so little action - but with a House and Senate against Obama, I'm sure absolutely nothing will get done for the rest of his term. The last thing I want to see is another government shutdown like last October - and a decisive government is critical right now with all the turmoil in the world. Russia is already riding roughshod over Ukraine, and I fear that's only the first step for Russia… and without a strong government to oppose Putin…

Oh well. No use fretting about it. But I think about these things, and wonder if anyone else does.

Anyhow, I voted. Then, as a reward for myself, I got a Carmel Mocha from the coffee shop in Inman Square. They were giving a dollar off for people who showed their "I voted" sticker. Of course, I would have gotten the Carmel Mocha anyway - it's become something of a tradition. Vote, get a Carmel Mocha. And it's always nice to get out of the house.

I wonder if I should try to talk Jim into staying up late and watching the election results? I don't suppose it really matters, as there's nothing I can do about it anyway, but I feel like I'd like to know sooner rather than later if the country is going to Hell in a handbasket.

Wednesday, November 5, 2014

Well, it's official. The Republicans were able to motivate more people to get to the polls than the Democrats - or maybe the Democrats have just turned their back on the party because Obama has become so unpopular - but the Republicans have gotten control of the Senate.

We're definitely going to Hell in a handbasket.

In other news, tonight was a Wednesday dinner night, and it was Jim's turn to cook for the group. I do love these Wednesday dinners - it's a nice chance to get away from the kids and be surrounded by adults, and a good way for our little group of friends to make sure we see each other often. And I'll admit it - I love showing off my cooking skills when it's my turn, and I love not having to cook dinner when it's everyone else's turn. I don't know what I'd do without these weekly dinners.

That being said, I hate when it's Jim's turn to cook. I get so crazy because he doesn't understand cooking, and can't even follow a simple recipe, so I have to sit there and watch and let other people help him, or else we'd get into a major fight in front of all our friends. I feel so useless, sitting there without lifting a hand to help. And he always cooks stuff that comes out poorly, or stuff I'd rather not eat anyway.

Tonight was no exception. He made nachos. Nachos, for a group dinner! At least it's one of the few dishes he can reliably make, but even so - I was embarrassed that it's what he chose to serve our friends.

Maybe I should try to exert myself a little more the next time it's his turn to cook again. Maybe I can help him find a recipe that won't turn out too badly - something I wouldn't be embarrassed to serve our friends.

Thursday, November 6, 2014

We finally met up with Gary and Becca for dinner. We've been trying to get together for what feels like months - between our Wednesday dinners and all the stuff we've had going on, and their difficulty with finding a baby sitter, we can never seem to make the schedule work out. Finally, we just went to their place and had takeout sushi in Arlington Center. By the time they put the kids in bed for the night, we had barely an hour or two to ourselves, and their youngest kept sneaking downstairs - I think she was thrown off by the the novelty of having us visit. When they're so young, I wonder if they even remember us between visits, it's so rare that we get to see them.

I felt bad about leaving our Ben with a sitter. We ended up not really having any time to chat, or play games, it wouldn't have hurt to bring Ben along. Maybe he would have had fun playing with Adam and Violet. I don't know why we don't get together more often, really - Ben is a little older, but not much, and it's so hard to find other parents we get along with well enough to want to spend an evening together. I should talk with Jim, and Gary and Becca, about setting up a play date.

Friday, November 7, 2014

We had our first CERT meeting tonight. I keep forgetting what it stands for - maybe if I write it down, it'll stick. CERT = Community Emergency Response Team. It seems weird to be affiliated with FEMA in any way. It feels very adult and grown up, and at the same time I feel wholly unprepared. I'm looking forward to learning skills that will be useful in a disaster situation, and it will be nice to have a role to play if something crazy should happen.

But on the other hand, I wonder - who am I to step up and say "Sure, I'll help people if a disaster occurs?" I'm really just a mom and a wife - and occasionally, a writer. With no college, and a very sedentary career, I can't help second guessing what I can offer, or how I'll even really serve in a disaster situation. One part of me wants to *think* I'd do well, because I've done well in emergency situations in the past - but I've also frozen in emergency situations in the past.

Oh, well - that's why we train. If I know what to do in a disaster situation, I can switch into autopilot and do it. It may actually be better that way - it'll give me a set of responses and maybe I'll feel like I'm actually coping with a disaster, instead of panicking or standing around uselessly.

After this evening's meeting, though, I'm feeling a certain urgency to learn some useful skills. I've been meaning to get my Amateur Radio License ever since we first talked with Dennis about joining CERT, so I guess I should really be using my time more wisely to study and get the license. And I keep telling Jim that we really need to get our FIDs so we can buy guns and start practicing. I do think I'd enjoy target shooting, and maybe being armed would be useful in a disaster situation, too. I guess it's time to step up my efforts.

Saturday, November 8, 2014

Another weekend, another day full of stuff to do with Ben and Jim and no time to myself. It's been a busy few months, and with the holidays coming up, it's only going to get busier. What happened to the days when I was younger and I used to get *so bored* because I couldn't find anything to do? Oh, for one of those days again.

Today was mostly winter prep projects, running errands, entertaining Ben - one of those days that just seems to be full of endless stuff to do that isn't actually any fun but all of it needs to get done. After we got Ben down for the night, I managed to convince Jim to watch an episode of that prepper TV show with me. At first, he was completely reluctant - I had to call on Wifely Prerogative to get him to agree to watch. But like me, he was surprised by how reasonable many of the participants are - they're mostly doing logical things to prepare for the emergencies they fear.

(Unlike me, though, he couldn't stop talking at the TV when someone was worried about a scenario that he found ridiculous. Particularly the civil unrest scenarios. He kept pointing out that many of the things the preppers fear have already happened somewhere in the world, and civil unrest was not an outcome.)

I think he's got a little more of a love/hate relationship with the show than I do. He seemed interested in watching more, but mildly perturbed at some of the segments. Still, I convinced him to watch more episodes - we ended up watching three before it got too late and we had to turn it off to get some sleep. And I did talk to him about keeping a few days worth of food and water on hand for our family, because of the real possibility of a legitimate emergency here in Boston. He agreed, so now I'm up late while he's in bed, looking up FEMA recommendations and trying to figure out what would be best for the types of emergencies we're likely to encounter.

Sunday, November 9, 2014

We went up to visit Dennis and his wife today, to help them work on their roof. It's only a small section of roof over Jennifer's bedroom, but this project has been going on for over a month. Ben went to a party with Jennifer, and one of Dennis' fellow officers was there to help - Thomas, a guy we met at the CERT interview and meeting.

I was pleasantly surprised by how much we actually managed to get done! I went with Dennis to pick up more supplies (he needed more flashing, drip edges and some hardware) while Jim and Thomas worked on getting the first bit of flashing up on the roof. By the time we got back, they were ready for the drip edges and the rest of the flashing, and with me measuring and cutting on the ground, and them working on the roof, we made surprisingly short work of it. We actually managed to get to the shingles today - and we even managed to get them all on! Now Dennis can be done with tarps, and all he needs to do is install the roof vent and a few other small details that he can wrap up without help. I'm so glad we were able to help him finish it, and I'm also glad that Ben had fun on his day out with Jennifer.

Now Jim and I can say we've put a roof on a house. I'm not sure if or when we'll ever use this skill, but it's an accomplishment and it makes me feel more self-reliant and less afraid of our own DIY projects. On the way home, I asked Jim how he felt about roofing after helping Dennis with his project… and he said "Whenever we need a new roof, I'll be happy to pay someone else to do it." I guess he wasn't as enamored of the DIY process as I was… but I'll remember this feeling, and what I learned along the way, and I hope we can use it ourselves sometime down the road.

Monday, November 10, 2014

Monday again! I can't believe the month is already a third gone. I feel like time keeps speeding up the older I get, and with the holidays now only a few weeks away, I'm definitely feeling a time crunch!

When I went to the store today, I picked up a few extra canned goods and non-perishables that I'll use to start our emergency food supply. It's just enough to get us through a few days, but living in Boston, that's all the emergency supplies we're actually likely to need. I can't see the power going out for more than a few days, and even in a major snowstorm like the Blizzard of '78, the store is close enough that we could walk there for more supplies if we needed them.

I watched a few more episodes of that prepper TV show today, and thought more about our emergency preparedness if something should happen here. With all of our camping supplies, we're actually in pretty decent shape if we should lose power. We can cook on our JetBoil stove or our gas camping stove. We've got plenty of headlamps and flashlights, and even a couple of lanterns - I just need to make sure I keep our batteries charged. We've got nice, thick sleeping bags and liners, so we should be able to stay warm enough at night even if the power should go out. Maybe it would be worth investing in a propane heater in case the power should go out during winter, but I'm not sure how much we'd need it. I'll think about it some more and run it by Jim when I get a chance.

Tuesday, November 11, 2014

A little over two weeks until Thanksgiving, but I'm not feeling very festive. If it isn't one bad thing in the news, it's another. Today, it's Russia. Last week, the rebel-held areas of eastern Ukraine held polls to 'elect' officials to independently govern these areas. Everyone has acknowledged that it's a farce - these elections weren't supposed to be held until December, according to the Minsk agreement, and Ukraine proper is decrying these so-called 'elections' as 'held at gunpoint' - really just thinly veiled opportunities to install pro-Russia rebels in positions of authority. And that's exactly what happened. Pro-Russia separatists were sworn in last week, and immediately news sources started reporting an increase in the number of military convoys passing into Ukraine. Given the volume of the convoys, it's impossible that Russia is just sending supplies - it must be sending weapons and troops into Ukraine. And why do that if they're not trying to grab more?

But now it has gotten worse. The BBC reports that a Russian submarine is having trouble in Swiss waters. The Russians deny it, of course, but Switzerland claims to have intercepted some distress beacons, and radar shows a submarine-sized object deep in Swiss waters. Russian craft, both water and air, have also been spotted further west - as far as the UK and Scotland.

I've been saying all along that Putin was just using Ukraine as an opportunity to dip his toes in the water and see what would happen. So far, all we've done is respond with economic sanctions, which Putin has laughed off or portrayed to his people as the wicked West punishing an already precarious Russian economy. The fact that he holds control of all the media outlets in Russia, and is spinning the entire thing in a pro-Russia, pro-Putin light, is disturbing.

It would be one thing if he was attempting to annex parts of Europe without the backing of the Russian people... but if Russia is behind him, we could be looking at another serious World War. Tensions are already high in the region, and it's been a while since they were relieved through war... it's been long enough that people have distanced themselves from the terrible price of war, and the possibility of it coming again seems more and more real, the more I hear about what Russia is doing.

It's also disturbing to me that the AP and other US-based news outlets aren't reporting half the stuff that's going on over there. The BBC has become my main source of news pertaining to Russia, which is obviously a lot more pertinent to the UK and Europe than it is here... so far. But if things get bad again, we'll have to intervene, and wouldn't Russia just love a chance to get us back for the Cold War and all of the ill-will that has stood between our two countries for decades?

Why does nobody else see this? The writing on the wall seems very clear to me. But no-one in the US is really talking about it, and I think it's something we should be seriously concerned about.

Anyway. End political rant. I'm not just a wife and mom - I'm also an informed citizen of the world, and these things really bother me sometimes. I can be more than one thing. I can have dimensions. Don't label me, stupid diary!

(Hmm. Maybe some stuff from my subconscious is bleeding off here... I think of myself as more than a wife and mom, but this little rant makes me wonder how much I really give myself permission to *be* more than a wife and mom. I should probably do some thinking around that.)

Maybe I should write down a recipe in my diary to counteract all this political musing... stop thinking and get back in the kitchen, woman!

Wednesday, November 12, 2014

Thank God it's Wednesday dinner. After the past few days, I was really looking forward to some relaxation, and a fun time with the group. This week was a takeout and game night, and I *needed* some mindless entertainment in good company.

There was another case of Ebola diagnosed in New York City today. I know all the things they say about how difficult it is to transmit, and how it's not contagious unless someone is showing symptoms - but this guy had never been to West Africa, and they couldn't figure out how he'd gotten it. Now it's being presumed that he must have somehow contracted it from the doctor who developed it after returning home from treating Ebola patients a couple of weeks ago, but if that's true, he got it in a public space… a space where who knows how many other people were also present. I'm not saying this is the beginning of an outbreak here in the United States, but it *is* scary, and it's something I'll be keeping my eye on - particularly as it continues to spread unchecked in West Africa, and we can expect more cases to be imported as the number of infected people grows there.

I started thinking today about all the ways someone could get Ebola if a contagious person was out in public. If the carrier sneezed on his hand, and then touched a gas pump, the gas pump would be contagious. If he rubbed his nose, and then handled money, the money would be contagious - and lord knows how often that changes hands. Door handles could be carriers, and shopping carts, and even walking where a drunk person has urinated could get the virus on your shoes, and you could track it into your own home.

It doesn't bear thinking about. I know it's unlikely… but it's not impossible, particularly not if it starts to spread unchecked here, too. And if it got into the schools? I know how bad it can be when things start to spread there - hygiene is pretty much non-existent among those kids, and Ben catches and brings home every case of crud that goes around. I wouldn't say I'm actively worried about it, but it is a frightening thought - so I'll have to keep an eye on how things go.

Thursday, November 13, 2014

PTA meeting tonight. Oh, how I hate those things. Sometimes I wonder how I get myself involved in all these activities. I was supplying refreshments again - only a few of us do drinks and snacks for PTA meetings, and somehow it always seems to be my turn again sooner than I expect. I made some of those mozzarella tomato basil kebabs, and some cookies, and supplemented with some store bought stuff - chips and pretzels and a veggie tray.

Karate mom was there. (Barb! I can say her name in my own diary, geez.) She gave me the stink eye again. I may have a new Nemesis. For pity's sake, lady - this time you can't be mad at me for giving kids sugar because this crowd is all grown-ups! But apparently chips and pretzels are full of horrible things because they're processed food, and the veggie tray wasn't organic, and the dip was full of fat... yadda, yadda, yadda.

Really, if I wasn't afraid of getting Ben un-invited to stuff, I'd give her a piece of my mind. But one must make nice with the other parents if one doesn't want one's child to become a pariah. I thought I was done with cliques and stupid school politics when I graduated high school... little did I know that I'd be in it all over again when I had a kid of my own, but parents play it on a much more subtle level. At least you knew where you stood when the other kids were little jerks - when you're surrounded by parents, you have no idea where the backbiting will come behind the little smiles and polite small talk.

Argh.

Friday, November 14, 2014

I'm glad it's Friday, and the weekend is upon us. I could really use a break from all these dire tidings. For once, I'm looking forward to throwing myself into whatever Ben and Jim have on the schedule. Maybe it'll be enough to distract me from all the bad news, and give me a little perspective. I feel like I'm becoming a pessimist, and I don't want that. I want to raise my son in a world of hope - a world where I can be proud that gay marriage is a thing, and racism is a distant memory, and feminism isn't a dirty word that invokes the anger of violent men. I want him to live in a world where everyone is equal, and everyone gets along - or at least where people use civilized means to work out their differences.

I realize that we're rather far from that world right now - the increasing acrimony in politics provides mounting evidence of that daily - but I'd like to think it's a possibility in our future. That in his lifetime, things really will be better.

I don't want to be focused on all the ways things can go wrong. But that's all I've been hearing about lately, and that's where my mind has been dwelling this week.

I wonder if there's a new Disney film out anytime soon? I'd love to go forget my troubles for a couple of hours, and smile at something fun and positive with my son.

Just checked - Big Hero 6 came out last week - maybe we'll go see that this weekend.

Saturday, November 15, 2014

Went to see Big Hero 6 with Ben and Jim today. We all enjoyed it, and it was a nice family outing. Disney may have produced a few flops over the years, but at least they can be relied upon to create family-friendly, positive-message-promoting cartoons and movies. There's not enough of that in the world today, and I feel like it sends a good message to Ben, as well as gives me a few hours to forget some of the negativity in the world.

We went for burgers afterwards, and then had a nice drive out to our favorite apple orchard for some cider donuts. It's getting a little late in the fall for this kind of thing - so glad we had nice weather today and could enjoy a family day. I want more days like these.

After we put Ben to bed, I wanted to watch a few more episodes of that prepper TV show with Jim… but I also didn't want to hear about all of the negative scenarios that the people on the show are afraid of. I just wanted a day of positivity. So instead, Jim and I spent some much-needed adult time together.

I can't even remember the last time we made love. It's not that I'm not interested, it's just that we're always both so busy, and so pooped by the time we go to bed. Some of the other moms say that if you can't keep your man satisfied, that's when he starts looking elsewhere, but I never worry about that with Jim. I know we're rock solid, and that he understands we're just busy. We always enjoy it when we do get around to making love. Maybe I should make an effort to get more done during the day, so we don't get to bed so late - and we're not so tired when we do.

Sunday, November 16, 2014

Jim and I had a fight today. It seems our good feelings after last night weren't fated to last too long. After lunch, I mentioned that I'd like to go to Home Depot to check out some heating options in case we should lose power at some point during the winter. I pointed out that they don't cost that much, and emergency preparedness for an actual legitimate emergency is worth the cost. He asked me to name the last time the power went out in the winter (I can't) and explain how it's likely to last long enough to need a heater. I tried to tell him that just because it hasn't happened in recent memory doesn't mean it won't happen, but he just got annoyed and didn't want to talk about it anymore.

I suggested he take Ben out to the park since the weather was still so nice today, and I consoled myself with some more episodes of that prepper TV show while they were gone. I agree with Jim that the things they're worried about are usually quite ridiculous, but the principal is sound. It is our responsibility to prepare our family for the types of real, legitimate emergencies that are possible and likely here in Boston. What kind of parent would I be if I couldn't feed our son, or keep him warm, in an scenario as simple and as realistic as the power going out? It's not like I'm asking Jim to build us an underground bunker to protect us from some imaginary civil war that will never come - I just want to protect my family from hardship in the event of a realistic catastrophe.

Obviously I'm still upset about it. I think I'll go bake something to help me calm down. Maybe I can find a way to foist off some cookies on some unsuspecting kids while Barb is around - just to tweak her nose.

Gotta find my small satisfactions where I can.

Monday, November 17, 2014

Oh, thank God for glorious Mondays. My client workload is low this week - it probably will be for the rest of the month due to the holidays. So I was able to spend some more time watching that prepper show again, and I started looking online to find out what other types of things preppers use to help them prepare for emergency situations.

Before this show, I had never heard of a Bug Out Bag (BOB - what a funny acronym!) Now I'm thinking maybe I should prepare one for us. I don't believe in civil unrest and giant EMPs caused by sun flares, but we could have flooding or some other emergency situation that would require us to leave quickly. Heck, we're pretty close to MIT, and they've had to close down the area from time to time due to hazardous chemical spills or gas leaks. What would our family do if they closed our neighborhood and we couldn't get home, or if we had to evacuate quickly? For that matter, what would we do in a house fire? I don't know what I'd grab, but it would be nice to have all the important stuff in a bag near the door so we could grab it and go in an emergency.

Of course, that leads to an interesting thought experiment. If we did have to "bug out" - where would we go? All of our friends are pretty close to the city, and neither of us has any family out of state anymore. Where would we go if we had to load everyone into the car and hit the road?

Hmm.

Tuesday, November 18, 2014

Jim informs me that we have a CERT training class this weekend. Because we're new to the group, they want us to learn where all of the supplies are for setting up shelters and dealing with emergency situations, and the proper way to load them into the trailer. Also, apparently they have a bunch of generators in the warehouse so they can provide power to homes where it's medically necessary in an emergency situation. Like if someone's on a respirator and absolutely has to have power to the home in a power failure situation, they can deploy the generator to keep things running. So we have to learn how to set up and run the generator, and how to maintain it throughout a crisis.

This reminds me of the whole debate over the propane heater that Jim and I had on Sunday. Jim asked our CERT lead how often they've had to use the generator to supply power in an emergency situation, and apparently it's not that uncommon. The last time they had to do it was in a flood situation this spring. So even something that seems unlikely to us, who are inexperienced in these sorts of things, actually isn't as uncommon as you'd think.

Food for thought.

Wednesday, November 19, 2014

Wednesday dinner tonight. This week, it's Mike's turn to cook. Unlike Jim, at least he can cook. But half the time, he wants to cook things that just don't appeal to me, and today's no exception. Why does everything have to involve cabbage? I hate cabbage. I hate the smell of it. I hate the taste of it. And the smell is going to be even worse this week, because I'm on my period, and all those hormones make me super sensitive to smells. Ugh.

My contribution to Wednesday dinner this week is some sort of Irish soda bread with caraway seeds. I think I'll eat a sandwich before we go, and I can nibble on bread while we're there. Oh well. Can't win 'em all.

Ben has some sort of big math test coming up next week before Thanksgiving break, so I've been working with him a lot on it. I don't know how Jim became a programmer when he's so crappy at maths, but the task falls to me. Thank God Ben's still in elementary school - I don't know what I'm going to do when he gets to high school math. My own bout with Calculus was quite enough to put me off math for the rest of my life, and they say that it just keeps getting more complicated. Maybe I'll even have a hard time coping with middle school math. Either I'm going to have to teach it to myself again, or take on some more freelance work so we can find him a tutor.

Really, though, Ben's not so bad at math when you explain it to him the right way. Sometimes he has trouble figuring out the story problems, but once you help him figure out how to unravel it, he's pretty reliable.

I should convince him to read more on his own. Our daily chapter of Harry Potter is going to come to an end soon, and I don't know if he's reading anything on his own. I suppose I could find something else to read with him, but I'd like him to be self-motivated like I was.

Before becoming a parent, I never appreciated how much kids are their own people - not just miniature versions of us, with the same interests, aptitudes and skills. I could almost wish he hadn't taken such a liking to sports, since Jim and I aren't sports people, but at least sports are good for team-building, communication and exercise. Lord knows I could use more of that myself.

Oh well, time to go start the bread and suffer through this week's Wednesday dinner.

Thursday, November 20, 2014

Time is not on my side today! I completely forgot that Ben's class is having a party tomorrow, and I promised to make some of those mini pigs-in-a-blanket that he likes so much. Plus I'm on deadline for a client tomorrow, and Thanksgiving is next week - I've got to figure out my shopping list and get to the grocery tomorrow before the weekend. If I don't make it to the store tomorrow, everything will be gone. It might already be late to start my Thanksgiving shopping.

No time for diary writing today - gotta run!

Friday, November 21, 2014

Oh. My. God. I am <u>EXHAUSTED</u>. I pulled it off, though! Super Mom and Working Wife to the rescue!

I was up until two in the morning making those stupid mini pig-in-a-blanket things, AND getting close to a final wrap on that client project that was due today. And of course, I was up again at six to start getting ready, and get Ben up and ready for school, and then back to work on my client project. I was done by noon - thank God for strong coffee, and plenty of it - so I made my deadline. Fortunately, that gave me enough time to put together my Thanksgiving shopping list and get to the grocery store before the after-work crowd arrived - but even so, it was mobbed! I had to go three different places to find everything I needed, because our Star Market was already out of stuff, and Whole Foods had too limited of a selection, so I finally found the last few items at Market Basket. Of course I had already gotten my produce at Star, and Whole Foods has much fresher produce... so I bought more produce at Whole Foods and now I have to figure out what to cook to use up the stuff I bought at Star.

But most of all, self, a word of advice: never go to Market Basket for groceries the week before Thanksgiving. Oy.

Managed to avoid a minor fender-bender in the parking lot when I got out, and stopped at Starbucks on the way home to treat myself because OMG I need more caffeine to make dinner and get through the evening.

With all the craziness the past few days, I almost forgot that my birthday is tomorrow! I feel like the older I get, the less I care about it. But it is an excuse to get out and do something. I asked Jim to take me to see Hunger Games - it comes out this weekend and I really like the series. Of course I forgot to book the sitter because I forgot this weekend was my birthday, but fortunately Jim had already taken care of it because he had planned for us to do *something*, even if I did forget.

I love that man. I know we've had some friction lately, but he's so sweet to me when he thinks about it. I guess I should figure out what I'm getting him for Christmas, but if worse comes to worse, me in a bow couldn't go wrong, haha!

Saturday, November 22, 2014

It's my party and I'll cry if I want to…

Just kidding! Had a very solid birthday this year. I feel like we maybe should have done something slightly more special than going out to dinner and a movie, but it was a movie I really wanted to see, and it was nice to have a kid-free weekend afternoon and evening - so I'll take it!

Jim and I had plenty of time to talk, and we were able to clear the air on the whole propane heater argument. He says that he understands I'm just trying to take care of our family, and the thing with the generators has shown him that even though he doesn't think something is particularly likely, it doesn't hurt to be prepared. I promised him that I wasn't about to go overboard, but I did use the opportunity to bring up the Bug Out Bag - he kind of rolled his eyes at me, but when I brought up the example of what would we grab in a fire, he nodded and went along with it. So I'll start looking into what should be in a Bug Out Bag, and what kind of bag it should be, and where I should stash it. Jim may roll his eyes at me, but I think he'll be grateful if we ever do need it in an emergency.

And then I can tell him ever-so-sweetly that I was right. Hah!

Bonus birthday gift? Early bedtime for some grown-up alone time. Wow, I needed that. Feeling so much more relaxed now.

What a pleasant day.

Sunday, November 23, 2014

Today was our CERT class to familiarize us with all of the equipment in the warehouse, how to set up and use the generator, how to load the trailer and what to use in what type of emergency, etc. I'll admit I was a little intimidated by the generators, and they are noisy, but they're actually pretty easy to set up and use.

It kind of made me think about what we'd do at home if we lost power - we'd lose everything in the fridge and freezer because we couldn't run it, and we wouldn't be able to charge our cell phones or any of our battery-operated lights and things. I got Jim to give a little on the propane heater thing - maybe I'll just look into generators when I get some free time tomorrow and see how much they cost.

Thanksgiving week coming up! Ahh! I've got to get as much stuff pre-prepped as I can, because Ben is home on Wednesday and I never get as much done as I think I can when he's home. Thankfully my workload is super light this week, so I can try to get everything wrapped up tomorrow. That would give me Tuesday to prep and cook, and then I'll be able to entertain Ben on Wednesday.

Super Mom is an excellent time manager! Sometimes, anyway.

Monday, November 24, 2014

Well, crap. I had gotten everybody off to school and work and was researching generators when I got an automated call that Ben's school has had an outbreak of norovirus. The message said they've got extra people in to try to clean and sanitize the school. I looked it up on the Boston Globe website and saw that over 140 students and 10 teachers are out sick due to the norovirus. That's practically a quarter of Ben's school!

He almost always gets sick when something is going around at school, and the last thing I need is for him to get sick on Thanksgiving week - or me, for that matter! - so I went down to school and picked him up. It's a short week, anyway - they were only in class today and tomorrow, and off Wed through Fri, so I'd rather have him do some make-up work than get sick - and bring it home and make the rest of us sick, too. I was able to get most of his work, although he'll have to do a make-up test next week for the big math test we've been working on - so right now I'm having him do some of his make-up work while I try to salvage my Thanksgiving prep. Of course this means even less time to get everything done, with him home from school all week, but I shall persevere!

LATER

Double crap. Boston has had its first official case of Ebola. They've got the person isolated now, and are working to track down who else might have been exposed, but they're not releasing any details about who the person is, where he or she worked and whether the person had traveled to West Africa lately. Technically, they're still waiting on additional testing from the CDC to confirm it's Ebola, but the hospital seems certain based on preliminary testing - and they've taken the appropriate precautions.

I know it's just a single case. I know it's unlikely that anyone else was exposed. But this is far too close to home for comfort. I'm afraid that if a real outbreak started, we'd have dozens of people exposed - potentially exposing hundreds more - before we even realized what was happening.

I know there's not anything I can do about it right now, and there's no point worrying until there's more information and a lot more cases... but I can't seem to help myself. Maybe it's time to get a head start on my baking and work out some of this nervous energy.

Well, Jim was annoyed that I kept Ben at home, but I'm not sorry. Even more kids are out today with the norovirus, and none of us are sick, so I think I did the right thing. Besides, Jim's at work and I work from home so it doesn't really affect him anyway.

Something worse happened today, though, and I think that's what's got Jim really annoyed.

It all started when Ben asked about Ebola. No, I wasn't talking about it, but... well, I'll just write down the conversation. Maybe if I ever pass this diary on to my kids or grandkids, they'll read it and do a better job if something like this conversation comes up. Or maybe we can use it to explain what happened to the therapist Ben will inevitably need.

"Mom, what's Ebola?"

"Where did you hear about Ebola?"

"Everyone's talking about it. They're saying it a lot on the news, and people on Twitter and Facebook are talking about it, but I don't really know what it is."

"Oh. Well, Ebola is kind of like the flu, only it's harder to catch - and it's more dangerous."

"How do you catch it?"

"Well, you know how we always tell you to use a Kleenex when you sneeze, and to wash your hands when you use the bathroom? You catch Ebola by touching someone's bodily fluids - like when they go to the bathroom, or sneeze - and getting it inside you. Like if you rub your nose or your eyes with someone's snot or fluids on your hands, or if you eat something without washing your hands, or if you've got a cut when you come into contact with infected bodily fluids."

"What about blood?"

"Why blood?"

"Some of the people who are talking about Ebola are talking about blood."

"Well, one of the symptoms of Ebola is you start to bleed inside, and then the blood might come out with your snot when you sneeze, or if you throw up or go to the bathroom."

"You said Ebola is more dangerous than the flu, and just now you said it makes you bleed. Why do you bleed? Why is it more dangerous?"

"Umm, well, it's kind of complicated, but Ebola causes the blood to come out of the blood vessels. If someone gets Ebola and doesn't get the right medical treatment, that person could die."

Yes. Die.

I heard the word coming out of my mouth before I knew what I was saying. We've never had the "death" talk with Ben. Both Jim and I lost the last of our family members when Ben was just a baby, so he was too young to be aware of what was happening. I'm sure by now he's probably encountered it out in the world, but we've never had a talk about it, and I kind of assumed Jim and I would handle it together whenever it came up.

Well, before I put my foot in it, that is.

Needless to say, I fumbled around trying to explain death after that. I was trying to figure out what to say that wouldn't be too alarming, but also wouldn't insult my son's intelligence. I haven't read up on this, and I have no idea what I can or should say to him at this age, but I'm sure it would be traumatic for him to start worrying about Jim or me dying, so… I tried my best. He didn't seem too alarmed, but sometimes it's hard to tell what's sinking in and what's sort of going over his head.

Of course, that wasn't the end of it. I thought it was - he got quiet after I tried to explain death in a non-traumatic way, and shortly after that he went back to his homework. But he stayed in the kitchen with me, instead of going up to his room, and when Jim got home, it became obvious that he hadn't finished with the topic.

"Dad, mom says that Ebola is more dangerous than the flu, but also harder to catch. I don't want you to die, so you should make sure you wash your hands a lot and don't rub your nose or your eyes - and make sure you don't have any little cuts on your hands. I guess if you've got a paper cut or something, you should probably wear gloves."

Surprisingly, Jim handled the unexpected bomb like a pro. He thanked Ben for the advice, and suggested that it was a good practice to wash hands regularly anyway, but that it was extremely unlikely that any of us would come into contact with Ebola, so he shouldn't worry about it too much.

Of course, I got an earful later. I tried to explain how it had come about, and that it wasn't me trying to scare Ben with stories of Ebola - but Jim seems to have gotten it into his head that I'm afraid of it, and that I was worried that the norovirus in Ben's school was actually Ebola, and that's why I kept him home.

Which is ridiculous, of course, but now that he's put that thought into my head, I find it slightly terrifying. The thought of Ben getting Ebola,

and watching him suffer and die a slow and painful death - it's horrific.
Or the rest of us, of course, but it's particularly horrifying to think about
it happening to Ben. He's so young. My baby. I can't imagine what I'd do.

Wednesday, November 26, 2014

So. Tired.

It's the day before Thanksgiving, and I've been running myself ragged today between trying to prep my contributions to Thanksgiving dinner and trying to keep Ben happily occupied. We've finished the last of his make-up work from missing school, and I'm still not regretting keeping him home, in spite of the tension between Jim and me. But that means Ben and I have had to move on to other things, and I'm strongly opposed to the type of parenting that involves plopping him down in front of a screen (except in small doses) so I end up being more actively involved in keeping him entertained throughout the day.

I was able to let him help me make some of the quick breads, even though it always takes forever when he helps. This year I did two loaves of Cranberry Orange Nut Bread, a loaf of Pumpkin Bread and a loaf of Cinnamon Apple Bread. I pondered doing cookies, too, because Ben loves cookies - both eating and making them - but in the end I didn't have time. I still have pies to make, and sides to prep… and those damn Parker House Rolls. Why do I keep doing those every year? They take forever, they get eaten so quickly, they mostly taste of butter and they're a pain in the arse. And yet, I keep doing them…

Got no sleep last night, and probably won't get any again tonight. I just keep going over lists in my head - things I still need to make for Thanksgiving, the order in which I need to cook the sides, what I can prep ahead of time and what I have to do day-of, and triage to keep my men from eating everything before we get to Ari's. Which, of course, means making them stuff to snack on so they won't touch the stuff that's meant for Thanksgiving dinner.

Maybe I should have made cookies after all.

Thursday, November 27, 2014

Thanksgiving!

There's always so much work and stress leading up to the day, but it's always worth it when we sit down to dinner and we've got such a gorgeous, impressive spread. I don't feel bad over stuffing myself silly - it's the least I deserve after all the work that goes into it.

And of course, I have so much to be thankful for. I'm thankful that we *can* put together such an impressive spread every year. I know there are people in the world who can't manage nearly this much. I'd love to volunteer at a food kitchen someday, but there's just never enough time between parenting and working and everything else.

I'm thankful for my wonderful boy. It's a lot more work than I ever could have imagined to raise a kid, but he's such a joy every single day - makes everything worth it. (Well, except when he gets into his bratty moods… but we're all entitled to a bad day every now and again.)

I'm thankful that we have enough of everything, and that we don't have to make too many sacrifices.

I'm thankful for my wonderful friends, and that all of us are in good health right now.

I'm thankful for my husband, even if we are having a rough patch right now.

Dinner is over, and I refuse to look at the pile of dishes right now - time to rest and relax for a bit.

Friday, November 28, 2014

Oh, the eternal cleanup after a big holiday meal. Guess what I spent my day doing? Surprise. Dishes. So many dishes. I know dishwashers are a luxury, but oh how I miss having one. If we ever move again, I've got to put my foot down and make sure we've got a dishwasher.

Jim was off work today, so thankfully he took over the job of entertaining Ben so I could focus on the house cleaning. They were gone for hours today - hitting some Black Friday sales and working on Christmas shopping.

Sometimes I kind of hate how it goes directly from Thanksgiving to Christmas shopping immediately. I definitely hate that retailers have started their "big Christmas shopping deals" *before* Thanksgiving now. But I feel like there should be *some* breathing room between Thanksgiving and Christmas. We just got finished giving thanks for everything we have, so it feels wrong to immediately go out and start acquiring more.

Jim might be annoyed about it, but I've decided I want to ask for some practical things for Christmas this year. Like the propane heater I've been eyeing, and maybe a generator. I also started thinking about what we'd do if we had an emergency and the water went out. Emergency preparedness guidelines suggest that you need at least one gallon per person per day for drinking and sanitation. For the three of us, that would be at least nine gallons for the minimum three-day emergency supply recommendation. Maybe I'll look into some water storage and water filtration options.

Saturday, November 29, 2014

That's not good. Another two cases of Ebola here in Boston. I saw an article about it from the Boston Globe in my Twitter feed, and then alerts started popping up from AP News and the NYT app. Of course, the three of us were having lunch together, and the boys wanted to know what was blowing up my phone. What could I do? I wasn't going to lie about it, and it's not like I've got an alert set for Ebola… it's just the news reporting stuff.

When I told them, Ben got quiet… but I could see Jim getting visibly upset. His mouth pressed into a thin line, and he got that wrinkle that he gets between his eyebrows when he's angry. It was obvious that he was upset about it, but he didn't want to say anything in front of Ben. So he just said: "Well, I'm glad they're in the hospital now so they can get the medical treatment they need to get better."

New details are still coming out - I keep sneaking glances at the story when the guys can't see me. So far, it looks like they're monitoring three hundred and sixty seven people who might have been exposed. Nearly four hundred people! Evidently the infected people were a couple, and they thought they just had the flu, so they kept going to work and going out in public until it got bad enough that they had to seek medical treatment and they were diagnosed. So they were contagious for possibly days.

I wonder if they took the subway? I wonder if they went to any restaurants? I wonder where they work?

This is far too close to home for my comfort. I know it's difficult to contract it - I just keep telling myself how unlikely it is that anyone in my family could come into contact with anyone who's carrying it. But I can't stop this panicked feeling deep in my gut that says I need to get my family OUT before it's spreading all over the city.

Sunday, November 30, 2014

Jim's barely talking to me. I hate it when he clams up like this, but it's hard for me to think about it too much when news keeps coming out about the Ebola cases here in the city. They've shut down both workers' offices for sanitizing, and they lived in a multi-family home, so they've had to evacuate, quarantine and shut that down for sanitizing, too. And they *did* take the subway and go out to two different restaurants, plus a movie theater, while they were experiencing symptoms - so they were contagious. Who knows how many people have realistically been exposed? How can they begin to track down everyone who might have been infected?

Ben is due to go back to school tomorrow, but the thought of sending him out into public fills me with dread. I know that realistically, the statistical likelihood of him coming into contact with anyone who may have been exposed to Ebola in these latest two cases is practically nil. But what if? What if one of the teachers was on the subway? What if the principal ate at one of those restaurants? Or, God forbid, what if one of the other kids was exposed? Last week's norovirus is evidence of how quickly things spread around school. I know norovirus is a lot more contagious than Ebola, but what if? Do I want to risk my son's life on a low statistical likelihood?

Of course not. I want to keep him home. I want to home school him, if necessary, to keep him safe. But I know Jim won't stand for it. He'll see it as me creating some sort of alarmist situation. As a rule, I'm not in favor of home schooling - I feel like kids should have a chance to interact with their peers, develop social skills, develop some independence from their parents, and learn how to respect other authority figures - school is great for a lot of things. But if going to school is going to endanger my son, isn't it my duty as a parent to keep him home where he's safe?

I don't know what to do. I don't want to get into a big fight with Jim, and I can't decide how much of my current panic is due to the media reporting new facts every thirty seconds, and how much it's actually a realistic fear. So I guess, for the moment, I'll wait and see. But I am damn sure going to start using all my free time to figure out a back up plan to keep my family safe, if things look like they're really starting to take a turn for the worse.

December 2014

Monday, December 1, 2014

If it's not Ebola, it's Russia.

But now it's both.

Russia is on the move again, apparently. The BBC reports massive movements of Russian troops across Ukrainian borders. Ostensibly, Russia still claims to be sending "supplies" - but news sources are reporting seeing troops and weapons in the convoys. And we're talking convoys that are hundreds of trucks long.

I know… I just know… that this is not an end game for Russia. It's just the beginning. The rest of Ukraine will fall, and then Russia will start marching across Europe. This seems a bad time of year for it, though - December is hardly the time for a ground invasion in Eastern Europe. But I'll bet Russia is going to grab something… maybe a larger portion of Ukraine, maybe all of Ukraine, but something more than what it's currently holding, and Russia will sit on it through the winter. By the time spring comes along, people will have gotten used to the idea and they won't bat an eyelash about it - beyond more of those clearly ineffective economic sanctions.

In the meantime, Russia will have used the winter to consolidate its position in Ukraine, and prepare to strike further into Europe proper. It will mass troops and weapons, secure supply lines, entrench its position and be ready to move when conditions are more favorable.

This is it. This really is the next World War.

It's not going to happen overnight, I know. But it's going to accelerate once Russia strikes outside of Ukraine - Russia will have to use some momentum to carry them across Europe - so we're probably looking at the next eighteen months.

And of course, that's assuming no-one resorts to the nuclear option.

All of a sudden, the world seems like a much more dangerous place. I feel like I need to do more than just have a few days worth of emergency supplies on hand in case we have a power outage or something. What if Ebola makes it unsafe to go to the grocery store? What if we go to war with Russia, and they start conscripting? What if someone does go nuclear - or use more guerrilla warfare tactics to destabilize the US so we can't intervene in global affairs?

I've been laughing at the prepper TV show people being afraid of unrealistic things - but maybe they've got the right idea.

I've started thinking a lot about the real types of threats in the world right now, and what I'd need to do to keep my family safe. I need to ramp up my own work stuff to bring in more money so I don't have to bother Jim to take whatever steps are necessary to take care of us. I know he's annoyed right now, but he'll be glad I've been so proactive when I've secured a place for us to bug out, and when we're safe from whatever bad things are about to happen.

After all, it's a mother's duty to keep her family safe - and I won't let my son suffer if I can do something to prevent it. Jim may not agree with me about what form those threats might take, but I know he'll see the sense in protecting our family.

Tuesday, December 2, 2014

I missed a School Committee meeting tonight. Jim was out with Ben at karate, and somehow I missed the notification when it popped up on my phone. I started getting emails from people after it was over. I know I should feel bad, but I was busy researching bug-out locations and looking at property online. It's hard for me to get worked up about what the school committee is doing when there are such serious threats in the world right now.

I've started working on a series of ebooks about emergency preparedness. Hopefully they'll bring in some money I can use toward securing us a bug out location and supplies. I've been looking at how much I can pull out of the retirement account and our savings, and it looks like we've got enough to put a sizable downpayment on a house, or maybe pay outright for a piece of property. I'd rather not involve our joint money, though, until I've gotten Jim onboard… we'll see what the timing brings.

Wednesday, December 3, 2014

Wednesday dinner night, but my heart wasn't in it. Normally I enjoy the break from routine and the chance to relax and hang out with friends, but this week I resented the time away from my research and my work.

I've been staying up late to get stuff done while Ben and Jim are sleeping. I'm almost done with one short ebook - now that I've made up my mind to write them, they're going very quickly - and I've narrowed down our choices of possible bug-out locations to Vermont and Texas. Although Colorado is tempting, too.

Vermont has the advantage of being nearby. Most preppers recommend that you pick a bug-out location that you can reach in a single tank of gas, in case you're not able to refuel. And Jim and I have always talked about buying a place in Vermont, so maybe I could spin it as finally acting on that dream. The problem with Vermont is that property is relatively expensive there, and it's too close for my comfort to major East Coast cities.

If Ebola is the threat, it wouldn't necessarily be easy to find a place in Vermont that's isolated enough that I wouldn't have to fear an infected person coming onto my property. If it's nuclear fallout, we'd be awfully close to Boston. If one of the larger nuclear weapons currently known was detonated in Boston, we could potentially be in the fallout area if the wind was blowing in the right (or wrong) direction. It's even closer to Montreal, which is another major city that could theoretically be the target of a strike (or an Ebola outbreak).

Texas seems like a better choice, both in its distance from likely nuclear strike sites and in the affordability and isolation of land there. But the problem with Texas is water. They've been having drought conditions for a while now, and collecting enough water to survive could be a serious concern. Also, I'm not thrilled with the government of Texas - their attempts to legislate women's health make me angry - so I'm not sure I'd want to own property there. Not that the government will be a particular concern if things fall apart.

Colorado seems like a good compromise. Land is relatively affordable there, and water is a lot more readily available. But it can be difficult to find a good, isolated spot. Apparently a lot of people start looking in Colorado and then buy in Utah or Idaho.

Obviously I need to do more research. So I resent the interruption of Wednesday night dinner. I'll carve out a few hours to work on my ebooks some more, and then in the morning I'll go back to my research on bug-out locations.

Thursday, December 4, 2014

I think one of my new ebooks should be ready for publication tomorrow. I normally wouldn't rush something to publication so quickly without time to sit on it, rethink organization, expand sections if need be - and of course, edit it. But I want to get things out quickly so it can hopefully start bringing in money. If I'm going to get us out of harm's way and keep us safe, it's not going to be cheap to do that.

I've watched another couple of episodes of the prepper TV show - just while I eat breakfast and lunch, and am otherwise too occupied to work - and I've started thinking about what I'd do if there was civil unrest and society collapsed. If an Ebola outbreak should really take off here in the United States, I could definitely see civil unrest spreading like wildfire. There'd be a run on groceries, and then the grocery stores would run out of food, and then people who are desperate for food would be raiding people's homes. And what if the Ebola gets bad enough to keep people from going to work? Critical infrastructure - like power, water and sewage - might not be manned. How long can the power grid survive without people going to work? How long can we keep getting water out of the tap, or flushing our sewage?

Maybe I shouldn't just be looking for places to bug out - maybe I should be thinking about some sort of off-the-grid home. Something with its own electrical and water supply, so I'm not reliant on infrastructure that could fail in a real emergency. Maybe something with a composting toilet, so I don't need a connection to a sewage treatment plant.

I think I'll try to carve out some time to research this more.

Friday, December 5, 2014

Well, technically I'm writing this early on Saturday morning, but I haven't gone to bed yet, so it still counts as Friday, right?

I got the first ebook in that series I'm writing uploaded to Amazon today. I have no idea how many of them I'll be able to sell, but if other people are getting as worried as I am about everything that's going on in the world today, it should sell enough. Any extra money I can bring in can go toward keeping us safe. Jim doesn't even have to know.

Jim's still barely talking to me. I haven't mentioned Ebola all week - thankfully, there haven't been any more new cases so I haven't been getting notifications about it on my phone - but he's still upset about last Saturday.

Speaking of which, I have no idea what to do this weekend. I really just want to spend more time researching bug out locations and off-the-grid homes, but Ben and Jim will be around all weekend, so there's no way I can really hide what I'm doing. And given how upset Jim is with me right now, I'm completely unprepared to talk to him about it. Now is not the time.

I guess I'll have to wait until next week to pick up on my research again. Although maybe I can tell them I'm on deadline for a client project, and ask Jim to take Ben out somewhere for a few hours so I can work.

But then, if I do that, should I work on the next ebook in the series I'm writing - or should I do research? The more ebooks I can get out there, the more money I can bring in... but money doesn't do me any good if I don't have a game plan.

It's getting really hard to balance everything right now.

Saturday, December 6, 2014

Today was kind of a disaster.

I decided this morning that I wasn't ready to start lying to my husband. It's one thing not to tell him about this research I'm doing, but I can't just lie to him outright and tell him I'm doing something else to get him and Ben out of the house.

Unfortunately, that meant I spent much of the day thinking about what I'd rather be doing - namely research - and not really paying attention to what I was doing with the guys. And Jim noticed.

He called me on it, big time. He waited until Ben was reading, (I'm so happy he's reading something on his own, even if it is just "Adventures of Captain Underpants") and then cornered me. He asked what was so important that I couldn't be bothered to pay attention to my son - he knows how to hit me where it hurts. I didn't know what to say, because I'm not ready to tell him about my research, so I just muttered something about being distracted. He kept probing, because that's what he does, and eventually I pulled the "I've been working late a lot and I'm just tired" card - true, fortunately, but a totally lame excuse, and I think he saw through it. But apparently that was enough for him to let it rest.

Now, though, Jim is doubly annoyed at me. We haven't really talked about the whole Ebola thing, and now he feels like I'm neglecting our son. I want to tell him that what I'm doing is FOR our son - to keep him safe, and Jim, too - but given how he's been reacting to things lately, I just don't think he'd see it the same way I do. I don't know how to fix it without lying to him, and I'm not ready to tell him the full truth…

So I guess I'll just keep doing what I've been doing: research when they're not around, and working on my own ebooks to bring in money so I can do the prepping without involving Jim, for now.

The thing is, I really *am* very tired, because I've been up until around two in the morning practically every night this week, and up again at six to get Ben ready for school. I don't know how much longer it's humanly possible to keep pulling this off. I'm starting to feel snappish for no reason, and occasionally I have a tendency to get weepy. That may be why Jim finally let things drop - I think I was tending toward weepy and he didn't want to feel bad for making me cry. But I need to find some better way to deal with things, because this lack of sleep is going to catch up with me in a big way.

Sunday, December 7, 2014

Just re-read yesterday's entry, and, well, that didn't take long to turn out to be true. Jim took Ben to play basketball at the gym today, and I was supposed to be making lunch, but I was so tired that I just went to lay down for a few minutes - just to rest my eyes and get in a short power nap.

When I woke up again, it was dark outside and I'd slept for around eight hours. I completely missed lunch and dinner. The boys came home and found me sleeping, and Jim decided not to wake me up. He dealt with lunch and dinner, and occupied Ben all day, and I woke up just before Ben's bedtime.

After we put Ben to bed, Jim was pretty quiet. He said he needed to do some work, so he pulled out his laptop and pretty much ignored me until bedtime. I was able to get some work done on my next ebook, but the atmosphere was horrible - it felt so very tense between us. I tried to thank him for letting me sleep, as I'd been so tired, but he just grunted and continued poking his laptop.

When he went to bed, I, of course, was wide awake thanks to sleeping all day. I stayed up for a few hours and did more work on my ebook, and watched a few more episodes of the prepper show.

Obviously I can't keep going like I have been. I've decided to focus more on bringing in extra cash so I can afford to do the things I want to do, and not spend as much time researching property and potential bug-out locations until I'm able to act on the research.

That is, unless something else happens that makes me feel like I need to speed things up.

I haven't heard much news on the Russia front, and I think that will be a slow process anyway. Ebola is more of a concern, and there haven't been any new cases since last weekend, so maybe I've got a little time before I have to take action. I'll just try to keep an eye on everything, and keep watching this prepper TV show to get ideas for things we might need, and hopefully I'll have enough money to get going before things get too bad.

Monday, December 8, 2014

I can't remember the last time I was so happy for a Monday. I just felt so bad after yesterday, I woke up early to get the guys off to school and work, and I made them an extra special breakfast. After staying up late last night since I slept so much yesterday, I basically only had a nap before getting up to send the guys off today.

Ben seemed to appreciate the smiley-face chocolate chip pancakes and sausage. Jim didn't really soften toward me, though - he kind of eyed me for a minute when I made him a plate, but at least he took it and ate it. I feel bad for neglecting them yesterday, but I don't really know what to do to make it up to them. Jim just seems to be adding more and more offenses to some running tally he's keeping in his head - I know he's disappointed and upset with me, but I don't think I've done anything *that* egregious.

After Jim left to drop Ben off at school, I scooted up to the office to get some more work done on my ebook. I couldn't resist anymore and checked in on my first one, and it's selling ok. Not great, but ok. Maybe once I get a few more of them up, I'll send some free copies to some well-known preppers and see if they'll review them. Or something. I suppose I should just be happy for any extra money I can bring in, but I'll need to make more than this if I'm to make a dent in buying property for a bug-out location.

That's really all I did today. Cooked, cleaned, cooked some more, worked on my ebooks. I didn't even watch any of the prepper TV show today. I'm trying to stop stretching myself so thin, because clearly I can't pull it off long-term.

Tuesday, December 9, 2014

Crashed hard last night by the time Jim got home from work. I had just finished helping Ben with his homework - last week's make-up math test didn't go so great, so we're working on some extra credit - and putting the finishing touches on dinner. Luckily it was a slow-cooker meal I started shortly after the guys left yesterday, so I didn't have to do much with it by dinner time. When Jim came in, I could barely keep my eyes open. I basically didn't talk at all during dinner, and all I could do to clear up was dump the dishes in a pile in the sink. I had to ask Jim to put away the leftovers, because I had to go to bed. I left Jim alone with Ben for the evening while I slept the sleep of the dead.

Apparently I've managed to completely screw my sleep schedule. I was in bed by eight o'clock - before Ben even went to bed! And I had such a hard time getting up to get the guys off to school and work this morning. I was sleeping so deeply that I didn't hear Jim come to bed at all last night.

Fortunately, after a rough start this morning, I'm feeling somewhat revived today. I guess I'll need a few solid blocks of sleep to make up for burning the candle at both ends for so long. I wish there was a way to get some stuff off my plate so I could focus on getting more ebooks done and figuring out what to do for prep.

Today was another semi-productive day. I was able to work on my ebooks for most of the day until Ben came home, but then we had to start working on holiday baking. I'm doing my annual cookie trade with Ben's play group moms, and with those ladies involved, I daren't slack off my game. Fortunately, Ben loves to help with our intricate holiday cookies (I think he just loves the decorating, but he also likes to help knead and roll dough - anything to get his hands messy, I suppose!) so it's something I can do *with* him instead of trying to get it done before he gets home from school.

When Jim came home, the house smelled wonderful and Ben and I were working away like busy little bees in the kitchen, giggling and making a mess and singing along to Ben's favorite Christmas music. I think Jim was happy to see it, because he smiled when he came in - for the first time in what seems like weeks. I'm not thrilled about taking the time to do this, but I'm glad Jim seems a little more favorably disposed because of it.

Jim took care of dinner, since Ben and I were elbow-deep in cookie dough, and we all snuggled up on the couch afterward and watched some of the Original Christmas Classics collection. Ben fell asleep while we watched, but Jim and I kept watching until we started getting sleepy. Jim carried him up to bed, and then we enjoyed some of our own holiday spirit before bedtime.

I've missed days like this with my family. I'll be happy to get all this prepping stuff done so I can go back to focusing on living our lives together.

Wednesday, December 10, 2014

Blah. Had to spend most of today finishing up the rest of the Christmas baking for the holiday cookie trade, so I didn't get to work on my ebooks or do any research. Delivered the cookies before heading off to Wednesday dinner, so at least that's one thing I can check off my list for this year's busy holiday season.

Jim was still in a good mood after yesterday, so I tried not to be too impatient with another Wednesday dinner taking me away from what I'd really rather be working on. Although after getting the cookies done, all I wanted to do was get down to work. I haven't gotten nearly as much done as I'd like to this week.

The closer we get to Christmas, the more hectic this month is going to get. In fact, the day itself is just over two weeks away and I haven't even started my Christmas shopping! Maybe I'll beg out of the next few Wednesday dinners until we get through the holidays. I hope that doesn't annoy Jim all over again - maybe I can tell him I've got more work to do and need the extra time so I can meet deadlines.

Which reminds me, I do have deadlines on two of my regular monthly projects on Friday, so I guess I'm going to have to spend the rest of the week doing actual work instead of working on my ebook project.

Where's a Time-Turner when you need one?

Thursday, December 11, 2014

I sat down this morning to do just a little work on my ebook project before switching to client work… and the next thing I knew, Ben was coming in the door and I'd lost the entire day. I had to switch gears to help with his homework, and get started on something quick for dinner - which means I'm on deadline for two client projects tomorrow and I didn't do any work on them today at all.

I'm kind of freaking out right now. I needed pretty much all day today to work on these projects, and I was going to have to work late tonight to get everything done for tomorrow. But now, since I lost most of the day working on my ebooks, I don't see how I can possibly get it all done. I haven't missed a deadline since I started freelance writing - it's one of my selling points when I pitch to new clients. How can I possibly make this up to them?

Wonder if I can get it all done if I skip sleep tonight? I used to pull the occasional all-nighter now and again back in the day - granted, that was before I had a kid, but shouldn't I still be able to do it just this once?

Friday, December 12, 2014

Well, that's it.

I've missed my first deadline.

Not only that, though, but the work I did turn in was sub-par. I almost feel worse about that than I do about missing the deadline.

I did manage to stay up all night to work... but unsurprisingly, sometime around two in the morning, I hit a wall. I pushed through, but every word I dredged up after that was crap. I tried, I really did, but I was rushing, and I was too tired to pay the usual close attention to word choice, and the writing suffered. Now that I think about it, I probably should have just not turned that work in, either, and missed both deadlines. At least then I might still have two clients upset with me, but I wouldn't have compromised my reputation.

The deadline I missed was for the law firm. Fortunately, the project wasn't mission critical, and I haven't missed a deadline for them before, so they were really understanding. It turns out that the firm is half-empty now, because of the holidays, so the people who would need to sign off on the writing aren't really waiting for it. I still feel bad about missing the deadline, but I may as well have just told them earlier I was going to have problems with it, and saved myself the stress.

The writing that I did turn in was for the SEO firm. I feel really bad, because it's for one of their clients, so the client is the one who will get angry with them if they decide my writing is as bad as it feels. I kind of hope they look it over before sending it to the client, and send it back to me for edits. They might be annoyed about it, but at least then I'd get a chance to correct it before they send it to the client.

It's late, and I'm a walking zombie. Need to get to bed if I'm going to survive a weekend without making Jim angry at me again.

Saturday, December 13, 2014

The holiday season is definitely upon us. From here on out, I'm not going to have a weekend moment that isn't filled with holiday-specific missions, and most of my weeknights are probably going to go this way, too. It's a good thing Ben loves it so much that I can't resist his adorable little face - maybe he'll pass on some holiday cheer to what has been feeling like a less-than-cheery world to me lately.

Ben had a play date today, and Jim and I were up next for kid-wrangling, so we got to take them to the laser tag thing they voted for this month. Two other parents were there, too, but it was quite a feat to keep an eye on all the little buggers as they were running around pretending to be characters from some post-apocalyptic movie.

Some of them had the idea of being members of some faction known for bravery, so they were jumping off things and doing crazy barrel rolls and all kinds of spastic gymnastics, and it's a small holiday miracle that none of them hurt themselves. Also, what parent lets a kid this age watch a post-apocalyptic movie anyway? I think Ben is a little young for that. Although maybe Harry Potter and Star Wars aren't much better, now that I think about it… I guess I should figure out what movie it is, watch it, and decide if it's ok for Ben to watch it. Although maybe that isn't such a good idea, after all, with Jim being all sensitive about me exposing Ben to "adult" stuff too early. What if a post-apocalyptic future actually isn't too far off? If we have another World War, it won't matter how old Ben is - we'll have to deal with it.

Oh well, these thoughts are way too depressing for the holiday season. I digress.

After play group was over, Jim decided it would be a good idea to go shopping for gifts for Ben's play group friends, since the group was fresh in our minds. So it was off to one of those mega toy stores, where we let Ben pick out what he wanted to give his friends. This is the first year we've let him shop for other kids - usually we just buy a handful of things ourselves - but he's getting old enough that he really wants to participate, and he went crazy over it. We must have been there for over an hour, and we ended up with a cart full of stuff, so we had to tell him to pick just one thing for each person and put the rest back. That started a little tussle, which was on the verge of becoming a major tantrum until Jim took him aside and spoke privately with him.

On the one hand, I love that my kid wants to give so much to other kids. But on the other hand, I'm not rich, and sometimes I forget that Ben isn't some mature adult capable of thinking logically about everything - he's still a kid, and today he showed it in the little hissy fit he threw. He's been so good in the past few years that I think I've started to take it for granted a little bit. Yes, he's growing up - but he isn't *grown* up - far from it.

It just reminds me again that I really need to take care of him, because he's far from ready to take care of himself. As a mom, I want to do whatever I have to do to keep my son safe. After the holidays, I really need to figure out what's a legitimate threat, and what I need to do for my family's well-being.

Sunday, December 14, 2014

I'm so glad that Christmas is in the middle of the week this year. If Christmas was on a Monday, there's just no way I'd be ready for it, because I am never going to get anything done on a weekend between now and then.

We actually didn't have anything to do for the holiday season today, so Jim decided we should spend some family time together. And for some reason, he decided that in the middle of the night, so he woke me up early so we could bundle Ben out of bed and spend over three hours driving up to the mountains in New Hampshire. Jim wanted to go to a ski area so we could play in the snow.

I love the man, but seriously? You woke me up early so we could drive six hours on a Sunday during the busiest time of the year - so we could play in the snow? Which we'll have plenty of before winter is out, without having to drive anywhere at all?

As much as I was completely perplexed by his logic, I've got to admit that I had a great time. We went to a place that has all kinds of winter activities, so we went tubing with Ben, and we rode in a sleigh through the woods, and we warmed up with hot chocolate - the whole nine yards. And yes, there was the obligatory snowball fight, where I tried to join Ben's team but unfortunately he and Jim ganged up on me. Sneaky boys. I guess they can't help sticking together - it's in their DNA.

Aside from getting up early and all the driving, it was pretty much a picture-perfect day. We had dinner at the little Mexican restaurant I like in Conway, and I got a Peppermint Mocha for the drive home - I couldn't really ask for more. (And yes, Ben is such a little trooper on road trips! Give him an iPad and a pair of headphones, and he's good. Either he's playing a game, or watching one of the videos we've put on there, or he's passed out napping. Thank God he travels so well!)

I'll admit, things feel really good right now with Jim. This weekend was so much better than last weekend, although I guess that's not difficult when last weekend turned into such an unmitigated disaster. I guess we really did make headway on Tuesday, and my efforts this week not to make Jim angry again appear to be paying off. I still want to spend more time on my stuff, and preparing for the future - but it's good to feel like my family's on the same page, and my husband isn't angry with me all the time.

Monday, December 15, 2014

Work crisis *somewhat* averted. I finished up the stuff that was past due for the law firm, got it off to them and don't seem to have done too much damage there. When I checked in with the SEO firm, though, they had already sent the content off to the client, so there's no chance for me to fix it before the client sees it.

I never thought I'd say this, but here's hoping the client has low standards?

I don't have much actual work on the schedule this week, and I know the closer we get to Christmas, the less free time I'll have (is that even possible?), so I'm going to buckle down and try to get the next ebook in my series out there. The first one seems to have gotten picked up somewhere popular, because all of a sudden it's selling a fair number of copies. I want to hurry up and get the next one out, and then I won't touch them again until after Christmas.

Work, work, work… but it will all be worth it if I can make enough money to keep my family safe.

Tuesday, December 16, 2014

Jim asked how work was going today. We haven't had much time to talk about non-holiday stuff lately, and he doesn't ask me about work specifically too often, so I was caught a little off guard. I told him I've been staying busy with my writing - which is true, but I neglected to specify how much of it was *my* writing and how much was for clients. Thankfully, he didn't ask what I've been writing about - I usually tell him if I pick up a new client, and I think he's gotten tired of hearing about legal stuff and the random things I write about for the SEO firm, so I didn't have to delve too deep into it.

Which is good, because I have no idea how I'd explain these ebooks to him. Thank god we both kept individual bank accounts in addition to our linked household accounts - I don't know what I'd do if he asked about why there's suddenly money piling up in the account. Although I suppose I might have to get tricky when we file taxes this year… fortunately I'm the one who prepares the taxes, but even so.

It makes me nervous and uncomfortable to be keeping something from him. Lying by omission is still lying, and it goes against everything I believe in for maintaining a healthy relationship.

But there's no way he'd be happy that I'm working on prepper ebooks… and that I intend to use the money to prep for our family.

I wish there was some way I could ease him into it, or some way to show him that it's not crazy - there really is stuff going on in the world that could threaten our family.

Wednesday, December 17, 2014

I've gotta stop saying stuff like that. It's like I've become prophetic or something.

Russia is becoming more and more of a threat. Russian troops are officially active in Ukraine - it appears they're attempting to consolidate their existing toehold and shore up poor supply lines and communications. It would be wonderful if Russia just stops there, but I don't see that happening.

Particularly as Russia has announced that it's resuming long-range bomber patrols from the Arctic Ocean to the Caribbean and the Gulf of Mexico. So, you know, basically patrolling around U.S. borders. Apparently Russia stopped this patrol practice after the end of the Cold War... and the fact that it's resuming again is extremely worrisome. Especially when a European think tank has been analyzing incidents involving forces from Russia, and they've identified forty dangerous incidents in the past eight months... including three incidents that could have sparked open conflict between Russia and the West. Even if Russia isn't openly trying to start a war, the think tank says that unintentional escalation is a very real possibility with this kind of brinksmanship.

The economic sanctions that the world has been levying against Russia are making an impact, in that they're hurting the Russian economy and driving down the value of the ruble - but that doesn't seem to be bothering Putin. It's hurting the Russian people, but the Russian media is blaming everything on the West - and the people seem to be buying into that. So as long as no-one puts the blame on Putin, he can weather these economic sanctions a lot longer.

Nato has been making noise about military intervention, but no-one wants another war, so they'll let Russia get away with a lot before they're really prepared to take action. And I've even heard rumors that Russia is prepared to use the threat of nuclear armament to deter Nato military intervention. So by the time people are prepared to stand up against Putin with military might, he's going to be solidly entrenched and threatening to use nukes... which means a deadlock. Another Cold War. And with this kind of brinksmanship, it's a real possibility that this one won't end as benignly as the last one did.

Needless to say there's no way I can go play board games and socialize at Wednesday dinner tonight. I'm begging out - I don't feel good, which is true enough, because this whole thing makes me nauseous with stress -

so hopefully I can finish my latest ebook. I can't wait for the holidays to be behind us so I can focus on buying a bug-out place and keeping my family safe.

Thursday, December 18, 2014

Crap! Somehow Christmas is a week from today, and I haven't started my Christmas shopping, nor have I stocked up on staples for my Christmas dinner cooking. In fact, we haven't even finalized what we're doing for Christmas dinner this year. I knew it was coming up - I can read a calendar, after all - but somehow I've been so distracted that I haven't really been paying attention to everything I still need to do.

Fortunately, I did finish my next ebook yesterday while Jim was out at Wednesday dinner. I spent today editing it and getting it uploaded, so now it's out there, too, and it can start making me money.

When Jim got home from work today, he said that Ari was annoyed that I wasn't there last night because we needed to talk Christmas menu. I've been emailing back and forth with him to try to figure it out - hopefully we can get the rest of it sorted tomorrow morning so I can go shopping.

I guess tomorrow is going to be mega-shopping day. I've gotta get my Christmas shopping done, buy some wrapping paper and bows and whatnot, and get to the grocery for all the flour, sugar, eggs and crap I'll need for the Christmas baking. And if we can narrow down the actual menu, I can buy that stuff, too.

Luckily, Jim mentioning the Christmas menu reminded me that I need to figure out what I'm buying for everyone. Normally I'd be done with the shopping weeks ago - this year is really catching up with me. So after Ben went to bed, I sat up and tried to find gifts for everyone on my list. I think I'll go simple this year - some sort of baked goodie and a smallish gift for everyone.

Hah. I used a pseudonym on my prepper ebooks - maybe I should get a handful of them and use them as stocking stuffers for my friends. Because the real gift of caring is pointing out to them what a dangerous place the world is, and helping them figure out how to keep themselves safe. Whatever material stuff I get them is going to be useless when the shit hits the fan.

Friday, December 19, 2014

Double crap. Last night was Jim's company holiday party, and I completely forgot. He texted me like an hour into the event to ask where I was and say he was worried about me since I hadn't arrived yet. I blew it so completely that I didn't have a sitter for Ben and there was just no way I could get there on such short notice.

Now he's annoyed with me all over again. He says I left him feeling like a fool, because all of the other husbands had their wives, and the guys who weren't married had their girlfriends - he was the odd man out. He said it looks really bad that I'm the only wife who didn't show.

I can't wait until I can show him everything I've been doing for our family. I know he'll understand and forgive me all these minor things when we're safe after SHTF. Just gotta try to hold everything together long enough to get through the holidays, and there should be a lot more free time after the beginning of the year to really get going on stuff.

Let the mega shopping day commence!

Saturday, December 20, 2014

Still shopping.

Sunday, December 21, 2014

Today I looked after Ben so Jim could do his shopping.

It occurs to me that there is entirely too much shopping associated with this holiday. I hate the consumerism, but not enough to risk pissing someone off by leaving them off my shopping list.

Exhausted.

Monday, December 22, 2014

It's the big week!

Ben is off school this week, so I have absolutely zero time to myself - I can barely squeeze in time to journal. I'm so glad he likes baking - he can help me get started tomorrow with pies and cookies to send to the office with Jim on Christmas Eve. Hopefully it'll help make up for me missing the holiday party.

And then, the Christmas cooking.

I'll sleep after New Year's.

Tuesday, December 23, 2014

Oh my GOD I love my son but sometimes he drives me crazy.

Home with the kid all week = a trial in patience. I need to find a way for him to burn off some of this energy since karate doesn't start up again until January, and the play group kids aren't around until the weekend...

Maybe it would help if I stopped letting him lick spoons, and looking the other way when he snags a chocolate chip or three - I'm sure the sugar isn't helping. But it's one of the things he likes best about helping with baking. Not so bad when I'm only doing one batch of something, but when I'm going all out and it's cookies and pies all day long, it adds up.

Maybe I'll put on some music and we'll have a dance party to tire him out.

(Why do I suspect I'm the one who will pass out after a dance party?)

Wednesday, December 24, 2014

Christmas Eve!

The cookies and pies were a big hit at the office, thank Jeebus. Jim still hasn't forgiven me for missing the holiday party, but this definitely helped.

I've spent the whole day prepping for Christmas dinner tomorrow, and wrapping presents with Ben - everything except presents for him. Gotta do those after he goes to bed. I'm so glad I'll have Jim home tomorrow to help with kid wrangling. Christmas can get a little hectic.

Home stretch now. Just gotta get through the rest of this week. Then one more week with Ben home from school, but everything will be so much more low-key next week - and he'll have his new Christmas stuff to play with!

Thursday, December 25, 2014

Merry Christmas.

I can't believe it went so well, after everything that has been going wrong lately.

Ben loved everything we got him. I don't know if Jim noticed that all of my gifts for Ben are self-reliance oriented, but Ben seemed to totally dig them. I got him a Snap Circuits Jr. so he could start playing around with wiring and circuits. I'll get him a slightly more grown-up version when he's a little older. May as well get him started early with wiring and troubleshooting circuits and whatnot, if we're going to have an off-the-grid electrical system we'll need to set up and maintain.

I also got him a Carnivorous Creations Dome Terrarium Kit. I wanted to teach him how to grow and care for plants, which might be a little boring for a kid his age… hence the carnivorous aspect. He totally loved that he could watch his new plants eat bugs. I think that'll keep him interested long enough for the plants to grow, which will be an invaluable skill when we're growing our own food.

The one thing I don't think Jim quite approved of that I got for Ben was a Daisy BB rifle. I want Ben to start getting used to handling guns and learning gun safety, but I'm not ready to go straight to real firearms, so I think a BB rifle is a good first step. The Daisy website said that they recommend the BB rifle for ages 10 and up with adult supervision, and Ben will be 10 in April, so I think it's close enough. If the SHTF soon, I want Ben to be familiar with firearms and prepared to defend himself in a worse-case scenario. It'll make more sense to Jim when I explain what I've learned and what I've been up to. Regardless of whether Jim entirely approves, though, Ben thought it was the coolest thing ever. Apparently I'm the awesome parent this year.

Jim got him the usual video games, Blu-rays, etc. Boring. More importantly, though, those won't teach him the skills he's going to need. Although, to be fair, Ben was pretty psyched about the video games, too.

I got Jim this year's version of the calendar I've been getting him for years now, and I finally got to give him the leather bag I made for him over the summer. I'm kind of horrible at keeping secrets, and I've been dying to give it to him since I finished it, so it was really nice to finally hand it over. He loved it, thankfully. It also saved me from spending yet more money on presents - I'm trying to be frugal this year so I can save as much as possible toward the prepping.

Which brings me to Jim's gift… he got me a few days at a writer's retreat, and a couple of spa day and massage gift certificates. He says that I've obviously been working too hard and trying to juggle too many things, so I could use a break - or a solid block of time to work on my writing instead of trying to do writing and family. It's a sweet sentiment, but that stuff is so expensive! All told, it probably adds up to close to $1,000. I'm wondering if I can trade them in for cash, and put it toward prepping, instead. Unsurprisingly, I didn't get the practical things I wanted - the propane heater and the generator. I don't know if he thought I was joking, or didn't want to encourage what he sees as an alarmist trend. Mildly disappointing, but not terribly surprising.

Dinner turned out amazing, and it was great, as usual, to get together with all of our friends in the evening, share a second dinner and trade gifts. And yes, I totally slipped the prepper books I've been writing into the stockings as stocking stuffers. They mostly thought it was a joke gift, but I'm hoping some of them will actually read the books and maybe it'll help them realize what's coming - and get them motivated to do something to keep themselves safe.

Friday, December 26, 2014

Ahh, the post-Christmas fatigue. Spent most of the day cleaning, but Jim did want to check out a couple of the post-Christmas sales, so we all piled into the van and went for a drive. We had lunch out, which was nice - we didn't generate more dishes for me to wash! Ben seemed to want to get back to his Christmas booty, though, so after Jim picked up a few things on sale, we headed home for a very low-key day. It's exactly what I needed after how frantic everything has been for the past few weeks.

I snuck onto my account and found out my ebooks have been selling really well! Apparently I'm not the only one who's concerned about what's happening right now. They've gotten mostly good reviews, and I think that when I add a few more ebooks in January, I should be able to generate a surprisingly robust income. Combined with what I've been doing to cut corners on our household expenses and squirrel some of that money away, I should be in a pretty good position to do some serious prepping in the next few months. By the time Ben's birthday rolls around, maybe I'll be ready to show him and Jim what I've been working on.

Saturday, December 27, 2014

Jim and Ben went out this evening to look at Christmas lights, and I feigned a headache so I could stay home and get started on my next ebook. I'm feeling really motivated after sneaking a peek at my sales yesterday. It's not NYT Best Seller kind of money, but it may be enough for a reasonable down payment on a good bug-out spot in the next few months. Just gotta keep cranking out these books - the more I've got out there, the more money I can be bringing in.

The new video games are already losing their luster, and Ben is getting into the Snap Circuits thing. I spent some time with him on it this afternoon. Maybe tomorrow I'll take him out shooting with his BB rifle.

Oh! I almost forgot - I had my amateur radio license test today. I aced it. They've gotta send in the scores, but I should be licensed soon, and that means I can start thinking about what kind of equipment I'll want. In part, it depends on where we end up for our bug-out spot. I guess I should probably hold off, but maybe I can spend some time researching various setups so I know what's out there and can more readily decide what's best once I have a location in mind.

Sunday, December 28, 2014

I told Jim I needed to get some client work done, and had him look after Ben for a while this afternoon and evening so I could have some uninterrupted writing time. I felt bad lying about it, but I really want to make progress right now - I'm in the zone.

This morning, though, I took Ben out to practice shooting his new BB rifle. He did very well with the basic firearm safety stuff I went over with him before I'd let him load - always point the firearm in a safe direction, always know whether the safety is on or off, know if it's loaded, etc. I think for the rifle, I'll get him used to unloading it before storage. It's not really a self-defense weapon, so it doesn't need to be constantly loaded. But in a few years (or sooner if SHTF before then) I'll get him going with a self-defense weapon, and that will stay live.

I did the good old "line up some cans" to shoot at. Ben loved it, and before long he was a really good shot! I may have to start setting up scenarios so he can practice moving and shooting, and maybe even hunting. It would be good to be able to hunt if the food supply goes down and we can't just go to the grocery store for meat. I haven't decided yet if we'll raise any animals, but hunting would be a good skill to have in our arsenal.

I guess that means I should learn to hunt, too. I can't get really excited about that - killing an innocent animal does NOT appeal to me - but if it means feeding my family, I'll do it. I do enjoy target shooting, so maybe hunting won't be so bad.

Yet another skill I need to learn ASAP. I really hope there's time for all this prep before things really go south.

Monday, December 29, 2014

Jim's back at work today, but Ben is still home all week, which means very little time for me to do my writing. Fortunately, I think I've figured out a way to carve some time out. I've made Ben a cool sort of pillow and sheet fort in my office, and I've made him a deal with some stuff he can do on his own. I've offered that he can earn an extra hour of video game time if he'll spend an hour reading, and a half hour doing something educational, like poking the Snap Circuit kit or taking care of his plants or something. And he can do that twice in one day, if he's good.

So he spent the morning doing the whole two and a half hour round - reading, education, video game - then lunch. We broke it up a little after lunch - reading, then we went and shot his BB gun some more, did some exercises outside and then came back and did education and video game. All told, I actually managed to get nearly five hours of writing time in with this arrangement! Ben was really good about it, and he seemed happy with the arrangement, too, so I think that should work for the rest of the week.

I'm so glad I figured out a way to keep him entertained and still get some writing done. Maybe an extra two hours of video game time, on top of the hour he already gets, is a bit much... but it IS his winter vacation. He deserves to have a little fun of his own, instead of working all week on projects and other busy work.

Tuesday, December 30, 2014

Snow! The first snow of the year (well, the first one with enough snow to actually stick around for more than a few hours). It wasn't a huge storm - somewhere in the neighborhood of four to six inches - but it was enough for Ben to get all excited (and me, too, if I'm honest - I've always loved the first snow). We suspended our little routine so we could go play in the snow. We were out in it for a couple of hours this morning, then we came in for a warm lunch and Ben actually passed out this afternoon for a nap. I must have been nearly as tuckered out as he was, because the quiet got to me and I decided to have a nap of my own! Aside from the time I accidentally fell asleep last month, I can't remember the last time I napped. It was glorious.

Ben wanted to go out and play in the snow again once he woke up, but I convinced him to spend some time reading and playing video games so we could save further snow-play for when Jim came home. I got in a little bit of writing before Jim got home, and then we all went out and played in the snow together. Why is it that the two of them always gang up on me in snowball fights? We should have kept going and had a girl to be on my side and even things out a bit.

Hmm. That's something to think about.

Wednesday, December 31, 2014

New Year's Eve! So close… this is the last big thing before life gets back to normal for a few months. But this is much more low-key than Thanksgiving and Christmas, thankfully. For this year's NYE party food theme, we're doing Mexican food. Jim's making his nachos, and I'm doing my Sopapilla Cheesecake Pie and churros. I think Mike is doing carnitas, and Ari is doing tacos… it should be fun. I need to stop at the store and buy some Mexican Coke. That stuff is so much tastier without corn syrup!

As usual, Ben will try to stay up until the ball drops, but I'll bet he doesn't make it again this year. He is getting older, though, so maybe he'll prove me wrong!

He is awfully old to be thinking about having a second kid. And if we had another kid, that'd be another mouth to feed and prep for. But if I'm going to have another kid, I'd rather do it before SHTF - while I can still give birth at a hospital and have medical care, and then have Jim get his tubes tied (or get mine done).

The last thing I need to be worrying about in a SHTF situation is whether or not I might get pregnant, and then dealing with giving birth without medical facilities. I doubt I could stock enough birth control to get me through the rest of my fertile years, and even if I did, it might go bad or get damaged. A more permanent solution seems appropriate, but if there are going to be any more kids, that should happen first.

Oh well, these thoughts are entirely too serious for NYE. It's the one night a year when my goal is to let loose and relax. Here's to relaxing!

January 2015

Thursday, January 1, 2015

  Zzz...

Friday, January 2, 2015

New Year's Resolutions:

1. Get a total of five or six ebooks out to bring in money for prepping.

2. Find a good spot for a bug out location, and buy it.

3. Set up an off-the-grid system for electrical and water.

4. Store up enough food and water for my family.

5. Learn whatever skills I still need to make my family self-sufficient when SHTF. (Agriculture? Hunting?)

Ideally, I'd like to have accomplished these resolutions by summer - I think Russia will probably behave itself until warmer weather, but there's no telling what might happen when the weather breaks. And a lot of this stuff is really ongoing - I should keep stockpiling supplies and honing my skills right up until things fall apart. But I'd like to be bare-minimum ready for a disaster by then.

With that stuff in mind, I think I'll consider changing up my journaling style this year. Instead of sticking with my plan of journaling every day, regardless of whether I have time or anything really interesting to say, I'm going to focus more on journaling about getting my prep done, and any other significant stuff that might happen. So I'm formally giving myself permission to skip days when it would just be the same old blather about work, Ben's school, family stuff in general.

Maybe. I do like having a record of stuff I can go back and look at later. We'll see what I actually end up doing.

Saturday, January 3, 2015

Holy crap my books are doing well! I changed up the descriptions a little bit and referenced current events, and the sales have increased.

More money, more prepping.

Mo' money! Holla!

Monday, January 5, 2015

I've made a decision about bug-out location. I'm going with Vermont.

Colorado and Texas may be better locations overall. But Jim and I have talked about buying property in Vermont for years, so I think I've got a much better shot at selling him on it. And I've been thinking about the various types of disaster scenarios that I want to be prepping for, and what I'm really concerned about, and it makes more sense to me to be close enough to get there on a tank of gas instead of trying to travel most of the way across the country.

Plus I'm really familiar with this part of the world - I know what I need to think about when it comes to long-term prep, I understand the seasons and things to be aware of, and I can actually drive out and look at the property before I buy anything if I stay here in New England.

There are a lot of arguments in favor of Vermont, so I'm making the call and that's where I'll be focusing my search.

Bonus? I'm using the research I did on bug-out locations and that I'll continue to do as I search for a good property as the basis for the next ebook in my prepper series - as soon as I finish the one I'm working on now.

Tuesday, January 6, 2015

Ask, and ye shall receive!

I've already found an amazing spot in Vermont that seems like it would make the perfect bug-out location. It's a farmette complete with a farm stand located on fifteen acres of land, just outside of the little town we love in Northern Vermont - Island Pond. There's a river on the property, that leads into the lake nearby - well stocked with fish. Good water source, nice auxiliary food source. It has pasture for grazing horses or sheep, so I could raise animals for food if I'd like. It's got a barn/garage, which I could use for a variety of things, from equipment storage/shop to something more farming-oriented if I decided to grow food and raise farm animals. It's beautiful and homey, with a pellet furnace that would be good off-grid heating (I'd just need to lay in an extensive supply of pellets - maybe I could add a wood stove) and there's a nice cleared hillside, so I could easily add solar.

In other words, it's hard to beat. The only way it could be better is if it was already off-the-grid (it's not, but I think I can add auxiliary systems) or if it was farther from town. I don't exactly want to be right next to a bunch of neighbors. But it's got enough land that I think it would be safe from casual contact, and if I get really concerned about security, I could put in some kind of perimeter.

It's a four-bedroom, two-bath, so it could easily support our little family - and even an addition, if I chose to have another child. It's not huge in terms of square footage, so it shouldn't be too much of a burden to heat. I can't help loving it from the description and the pictures.

And the best part? It's only $139,000 - and it's been on the market for over a year, and has had two price drops, so I think it's safe to assume the sellers should be fairly motivated. Even at full asking price, I'd only need to come up with $28,000 to pay a 20% downpayment and avoid PMI - which is definitely do-able. Between what I've got in my savings account, plus the money my new ebooks are bringing in, plus what I expect to get on our tax return, I could easily come up with $20,000. I could maybe borrow the rest from Jim, or maybe even borrow from our retirement account - one of the conditions under which you can borrow from it is to buy a house.

Even better - with the money I'm bringing in from the new ebooks, I could pay the monthly mortgage payment on this property three times over. If Jim wanted to quit his job and move the family up there full time,

I could support us. Although it would be better if he kept his job and we could use the money for prepping.

Anyway, I've emailed and left a voice mail with the real estate agent about setting up a time to see it.

Thursday, January 8, 2015

I've heard back from the realtor, and I can set up a viewing for the property next week. Just as well, as it's a three-and-a-half hour drive each way, which means I'm going to have to find someone to look after Ben after school, and I'm going to have to time it very carefully to get home before Jim does. Fortunately, it'll be a reverse commute - leaving the city during morning rush hour and coming back into it at evening - so I shouldn't have to worry too much about traffic.

There is a chance of more snow coming next week, so hopefully it doesn't prevent me from getting up there to view the property.

Tuesday, January 13, 2015

Well, for a fifteen-acre property, it's awfully close to the nearest neighbors. The buildings proper are right up to the road, and the closest neighbor is only a few hundred yards down the street. It looks like most of the property associated with the house extends along the street in the opposite direction - there isn't another neighbor that way for quite some time. It does go back a little ways from the road, but not as far as I'd like - and with the buildings fronting right up on the road, security would be difficult, if not impossible.

As much as I love the property, and think it's very affordable, I just don't think it's right for a bug out location. I want something a little more isolated to make it less likely that people will accidentally stumble across the house - and the supplies. Looks like I'm going to have to wait and keep an eye out. Maybe I should consider an empty lot, if it's sizable enough, and build where and how I want. But building would add a lot of cost, and time - which isn't consistent with my desire to get things ready for emergency bug-out this year.

In other news, Ben is really getting into the Snap Circuit kit. Snap Circuits has some bigger kits that are suitable for kids eight and up, so I think I might surprise him with one of those. If he really takes to it, maybe I'll get him the 300-In-One Electronic Science Lab. It's pretty pricey, and is recommended for ages twelve and up, but he does seem to be really enjoying it. Maybe I'll get him the more advanced kit for his birthday in April - he'd feel so proud of himself for using a twelve-plus toy when he's only ten.

Friday, January 16, 2015

I've finished the next ebook in my series, the one I started in December, and posted it for sale. Now I've got three up for sale, and the next one I work on is going to be about bug-out locations. Since I've already done the research on that one, it should go fairly quickly. I'm hoping to get it up by the end of the month.

I've been poking around electronic science toys for kids, and I've discovered that they've got a couple of solar educational kits. That would give him a great head-start on the solar power system I intend to have at our bug out location. I've ordered the more advanced of the solar kits, so now I just have to find an excuse to give it to him. I'll have to see if he has any tests or anything coming up, and maybe I could use this surprise gift as a reward for doing well on a test. Jim couldn't argue with that. They've also got a short wave radio kit, which could be a good introduction for Ben to amateur radio, so maybe I'll get that, too.

Tuesday, January 20, 2015

I've been putting off writing about this, because I don't really know how I feel about it yet. I guess that's one of the benefits of doing daily journal entries - you can write whatever you want without having to fully internalize it and figure out what you feel. Doing it this way, I feel like I need to have it all neatly sorted before I record it, but I miss out on the fact that writing it down helps me to work through it.

Anyway, I talked with Jim a few days ago about possibly having another child. I didn't present it as a "I definitely think we should do this" sort of thing - just tried to put out feelers to see how he'd feel about it before we talked further. I wasn't really sure then whether I wanted to do it or not, but I've been leaning toward it, so it seemed like a good idea to raise the topic with him.

It did not go well.

Jim brought up a whole bunch of stuff as arguments against having another child. He pointed out that I've seemed distracted for the past few months - which I have to admit is true - and how would I manage with another kid? He brought up all of the events I've been missing, from his holiday party (I guess he's still holding a grudge about that one) to one of Ben's karate tournaments (I do feel really bad about missing that one) to PTA meetings... ok, so I can't argue that I've been missing those things.

But it's just because I've been so focused on all of the things I need to do to keep our family safe. I'm missing those things *because* I love him and Ben so much, and I can't imagine what I'd do if I had to watch them suffer and die. So I feel like it's my responsibility to do whatever is necessary to keep them safe. And since Jim isn't onboard right now, I have to try to juggle everything by myself until I can reach critical mass and convince him of the value of what I'm doing.

I'm sure that once I have a bug out base, and some basic supplies, and can really sit him down and explain why I'm doing this, he'll be so glad I've been spending so much time on this. When that happens, I know he'll understand and he'll be 100% supportive of everything I've been doing - and hopefully, he'll even want to help. So I just have to try to keep things going until then.

Anywho, after he brought up all the things I've been missing, he really hit me where it hurts. He said that he feels like I've been keeping things from him. He says I don't talk to him much these days about what I've been doing - which is true, because what I've been doing is mostly stuff I don't think he'd approve of right now. And he said he feels like there's something going on because I can't be honest with him. To which I could only reply with silence, because he's right… and of course when I didn't argue with him, he knew he was right. It was horrible. I felt all the blood rush to my face and it felt like my heart stopped beating when his expression went slack and he turned away from me. I knew right then that the conversation was over, but for some reason I couldn't let it drop.

I tried to redirect, saying that maybe having another child would help us feel closer again, and would help bridge those gaps he was talking about - but he cut me off. I've never heard his voice so cold. He said he couldn't even think about having another kid until we could fix what was wrong between us. And that we couldn't do that until I was prepared to be honest with him. Before I could even think to say anything in response, he left - walked right out the door and was gone for hours.

This happened on Sunday, and he's been pretty cold toward me since then. I think Ben has picked up that something isn't right, but he hasn't said anything about it yet. Jim just comes home after work, tries to talk pleasantly with Ben at dinner while simultaneously ignoring me, then spend some time with Ben before bed - and after Ben goes to bed, Jim hides behind an iPad or his laptop or his Kindle and completely ignores me. And the cold shoulder extends to bedtime, too.

I don't know how I feel about all of this. On the one hand, Jim is totally justified in the things he's been saying, and in feeling hurt because I can't be a hundred percent honest with him. But the only reason I'm not being a hundred percent honest with him is that when I've tried to talk to him about being prepared for emergencies, he's been dismissive, or has even accused me of being alarmist and shut me down. So I feel like I'm damned if I do, damned if I don't.

I'm wondering if I just keep pretending everything is ok, things will blow over. Maybe if I can get better about not missing events and things, and can seem less distracted. But the more he pushes me away, the more I just want to focus on this prepping and get it done already so I can explain everything and get Jim onboard.

I don't know what to do.

Friday, January 23, 2015

Keeping my head down. Working on my ebooks during the day, trying to be the perfect wife and mother at night. Just trying to remind Jim of what we have… and if nothing else, maybe he'll soften a bit when he sees that I'm not neglecting Ben at all - in fact, quite the contrary. I've set up a couple of get togethers with his play group for the next few weeks, and I gave him that solar power kit as a reward for acing his English test. As I suspected, Ben totally dug it. He's really getting into all of this electrical stuff. Maybe it'll get him more interested in math. We've been working on improving his math, and he's got another test coming up next week… maybe if he does well, Jim will see that we've really been working hard at it and give me a break.

Tuesday, January 27, 2015

Still looking at property in Vermont. I've expanded my search to undeveloped parcels of land, as long as they're at least in the fifteen acre or more range. If I don't find something promising by mid-February, I think I'll start calling realtors. I'd like to have something secured by March, if possible.

Ben's math test is Thursday. We've been working really hard at it and I think he'll do well. He had an awesome time at the play group outing I arranged for the past weekend - he came home and couldn't stop talking about it to his dad. Jim has thawed ever-so-slightly, but still isn't talking to me beyond stuff pertaining to Ben. I'll take it. It feels like progress.

Friday, January 30, 2015

Ben's math test was yesterday, and I think he nailed it. We worked so hard at it this week, and I even got Jim to play a few of those math-related games with us on the Wii - Teach Math with the Wii and Big Brain Academy. I definitely sense a thawing from Jim, so I have hope that in time I can remind him how awesome we are as a family.

But it's been so hard.

I've had to really scale back the work I've been doing on my ebooks, as well as dramatically reduce the amount of time I've been spending on my real estate hunt. These priorities are so important to me, because this is how I'm going to keep my family safe, long-term - but it's useless if I can't keep my family together in the short term. I really don't know how to balance it all. Maybe the answer would be to talk to Jim about what I'm trying to do, but he's been so negative whenever I've even hinted at anything related to preparing for the unexpected. I think he thought the "prepper" thing was a short phase and I'd get bored with it, so I'm afraid to let him see how much I've taken it to heart.

I really wish I had someone to talk to about all this, who could help me decide how much to share with Jim, and how to approach it all.

In the meantime, I'm still trying to make gestures to spend time with him and remind him of what we have. Rush is touring again this year, and tickets went on sale today, so I grabbed some. We missed our chance to see Rush a few years ago when they were in Boston - I don't even remember why, but I think I didn't have a good sitter for Ben at the time or maybe he had some event or something. But it's something we talked about doing back then, and we were both disappointed that we missed it. Maybe doing something together, just the two of us, will help get things back on track.

Just wish the concert was sooner than June. Who knows what will happen between now and then?

February 2015

Monday, February 2, 2015

Groundhog Day. Man, I feel like I'm reliving some recent nightmare.

Jim is royally pissed at me again. Seriously, unabashedly pissed.

I missed picking up Ben today.

It really was totally, completely my fault. I was working on my latest ebook, and I was completely in the zone. I was researching stuff and writing away (and making really good progress, might I add) but I didn't set an alarm or anything, and I completely forgot that Ben had karate today. He gets a ride from school to karate practice with his friend Levi, but I'm supposed to pick him up when it's done. And I completely flaked.

I didn't really realize it was Monday, I completely forgot I had to pick up Ben today, I lost track of time because I was in the zone and just hyper focused… but I forgot to pick up my son.

And I had my cell phone in airplane mode so I wouldn't get constant interruptions from email notifications and news notifications and everything else.

Which meant the karate place couldn't reach me, and they had to call Jim. Who had to leave work to come pick up Ben, who sat there for nearly an hour waiting for one of his parents to come and get him.

I really did screw up. I have zero excuse. I have no desire to deny I messed up big time.

But Jim will not let me live it down.

He was absolutely livid when he got home. Of course he wasn't able to reach me with my phone in airplane mode, so the first I heard of it was when he and Ben unexpectedly showed up at home. I looked at the time and saw that Jim shouldn't even be out of work yet, and then I realized what had happened.

When I spun around in my desk chair, Jim was standing in the door of my office.

"You're not dead," he noted, his tone quiet but icy. I couldn't even speak, so I just shook my head.

"You're not unconscious," was his next observation. Obviously. I didn't even bother to nod.

"Has your phone been stolen? Dropped in the toilet? Battery dead?"

I cringed and held it up, showing him that it was perfectly fine but in airplane mode.

"Right then," he said, his shoulders drooping. It was that defeated look that made me feel even worse than the icy tone. It was like he had lost all hope and just given up. "I've got to get back to the office - I had to leave early to pick up our son because his mother didn't show up." He wouldn't meet my eyes. "Can you be trusted to feed him while I work late?"

I stood up from my chair and followed him out of the room, because I still wasn't able to speak. It was absolutely clear that there was nothing I could say that would make him less angry. And the truth is, I was angry with myself - I couldn't believe I'd let my son down so badly. This is the first time I've ever done anything so irresponsible.

If it had happened out of the blue, as an isolated event, when nothing else was bad, Jim probably would have been upset at the time, but then laughed it off later. It's not like no-one else in the history of parenthood was ever late picking up their child. But Jim has been angry and on edge for weeks now… maybe even months, so I'm afraid he's going to see this as a last straw. Proof that he was right. And I wouldn't even blame him - I can see why he'd think that.

Jim went back to work, and I made Ben his favorite dinner - that spaghetti sauce he really loves, and then we made cookies together for dessert. I told him I was sorry that I'd been late and that dad had to come pick him up, and Ben seemed to let it go pretty easily. But he did have a worried look in his eye when Jim left without saying a word to me, and he seemed upset at bedtime that Jim wasn't home yet. I've been trying my best to keep him out of things, but it's clear he's picking up that something is off with Jim and me. I'm going to have to talk to Jim about it, because no matter what's going on with us, I know neither of us would want Ben to be so worried.

Thursday, February 5, 2015

Things are worse than I realized. Jim has barely been around, and he's been making it a point when he is around to only spend time with Ben and I together. I can't get him alone for a conversation.

He got home super late on Monday night, and I didn't feel like it was a good idea to bring things up then, so I pretended to be asleep. On Tuesday, I was awake before him, but by the time he came down Ben was already up, and he took Ben to school - even though it meant he got to work earlier than normal - so I didn't see him again until after work. When Ben was already home. He went to bed right after we got Ben down Tuesday night - when I tried to talk to him, he snapped at me, pointing out that he'd gotten home really late Monday - thanks to my irresponsibility - and he needed to get to sleep. Wednesday morning was a repeat, and Wednesday night he didn't even come home after work - he just went straight to dinner with the friends, and then went to bed immediately when he got home.

Obviously he's not ready to talk, but I know Ben is picking up on this stuff, and I can't let some strain between Jim and me make our son nervous or scared. I need to get him to sit down and hash things out. I know I screwed up, but we've got to find a way to move forward and get past this incident.

In brighter news, I'll have another ebook ready for publication tomorrow. At this point, my ebooks are bringing in a fair amount of money every week. I can completely quit working for my old clients, and I've got a good chunk of cash saved for a downpayment on a bug out property, if I can ever find the right one. Between what I've come up with from my writing, and borrowing some from our retirement account, I might even be able to pay cash for a property and not carry any debt. That would be great news, and then I'd have something positive to share with Jim - and he'd see why I've been working so hard and what I've been trying to accomplish. I just know that once I have something concrete to show him, he'll forgive me and things will be good again, even if he isn't fully onboard with the prepper thing.

Friday, February 6, 2015

I suggested that Ben go spend the night at Levi's tonight (without telling Jim), so when Jim got home, Ben wasn't around. I made him sit down and talk.

That didn't go well.

I don't even want to repeat the things he said to me. Hurtful, accusatory things - things I'd never imagine in a million years I'd hear from the man I loved and the father of my child.

But then he started saying the scary things. Things about how he didn't know how to make things work anymore, and about how maybe it was time to think about changing the family dynamic.

I've always thought it was a cliche when people say things like "my blood ran cold" or "I felt like someone walked over my grave" - but that's how I felt when Jim started talking like that. I was simultaneously nauseous and lightheaded - like if I hadn't been sitting down, I might have fallen down. The blood rushed into my face, and my ears started burning - it was like the worse trouble I'd ever gotten into as a child, multiplied by a million. I honestly never knew my body could have a physical reaction like that. It's something I don't ever want to feel again in my life.

Even now, after all this has passed and I've had a little time to begin to process, I feel weak and shaky and just... off. Sad. Scared. Incredibly anxious. And completely spent, like I've run a marathon without eating or drinking anything - I feel all empty and dull and just... done. Crashed.

He didn't say the word 'divorce' or even 'separation' - but I know that's what he's hinting at. He did say that since Ben wasn't going to be around, he might go spend the night at Ari's - get some distance to cool off.

Honestly, at that point I didn't begin to know what to say. I was completely flabbergasted by the things he'd been saying. Even now, I'm not sure how I should have responded. You know how later, when you get some time to think, you come up with the perfect thing you should have said in a situation? I've got nothing.

But in that moment, I started to go from flabbergasted to angry at the hurtful things he threw around. If he only knew how hard I'm working to protect and provide for him and Ben, he wouldn't begin to talk to me like that. But I'm not ready to tell him yet - not until I have something to show him - so I kept my mouth shut. Between my stupid pride and my genuinely being caught off-guard, I had literally nothing to say.

And he left.

It's really, really weird not having him around. He's gone on business trips since we've been together, but this is the first time he's ever not spent the night with me for any reason other than being out of town on business. The house feels so empty without him and Ben. I know they're both gone every day with Jim at work and Ben at school, but this feels different. It's like the comforting walls of my family's home are now throbbing with anger and malevolence, and it's partly my fault but I don't know to fix it, but it's also Jim's fault for not being more reasonable…

I don't like it.

It's clear to me that I really need to find a place soon so I can buy our bug out property and then share what I've been doing with Jim. I have to fix things between us - this has gotten so much more out of hand than I ever could have imagined.

Tomorrow morning, I'll start calling realtors. I can't afford to wait until spring to expand my search. I need to make this happen ASAP, or my marriage might actually be in trouble.

Monday, February 9, 2015

That was the weirdest weekend ever.

Ben had so much fun at Levi's on Friday night that he asked if he could stay Saturday night, too. After making sure Ben wasn't wearing out his welcome with Levi's parents, I said he could. And when I told Jim, he decided to spend another night at Ari's. So I didn't see either of my guys until Sunday night.

Jim played it cool during dinner, and afterward, when we helped Ben with his homework and did the usual Sunday night routine of getting ready for the week. And after we put Ben to bed, he went immediately to bed himself, and didn't really talk to me last night or this morning.

And that was it. No further discussion. No talk about what we're going to do going forward. I haven't even had a chance to share my concerns with Jim that Ben is picking up on the trouble between us. He just won't let me have a conversation with him.

Valentine's Day is on Friday. We haven't made any plans. This would be the first year we didn't do anything at all for Valentine's Day. We tried skipping V-day once, before Ben was born - I tried playing it cool and making like the fake commercialized holiday meant nothing to me. But I was completely falling apart by five o'clock on the day, so we made a promise then and there that we'd always celebrate Valentine's Day, even if it was a fake commercialized holiday. We were supposed to take turns planning for it - this year was supposed to be his year. I have no idea if he's made any plans, and I haven't had a chance to ask him. But since he won't even talk to me, I assume we're going to miss it this year.

That hurts me more than I can say.

Tuesday, February 10, 2015

I wasn't able to get ahold of too many realtors on Saturday - apparently they're mostly busy with open houses and showings and stuff on the weekend - so I've been spending a lot of time on the phone yesterday and today, trying to find some property options, or at least a brokerage firm that I like.

It turns out, there's not really too much that would meet my needs. But I did find a realtor at one brokerage firm that really seemed to understand what I was looking for. He said that off-the-grid properties with decent parcel size did come on the market, from time to time, but that there's pretty low turnover in that type of property, because the people who build them tend to stay for a long time once they get set up. It's understandable, given that you have basically no bills (cable internet?) and you can grow your own food. He also said that when places like that do sell, they don't always go through brokerage firms - they may get sold through word of mouth within certain communities to avoid brokerage fees and ensure they go to like-minded folk. He promised to keep an ear open for me, though, and said he'd check on a few listings that might be workable. So I have hope, now.

I really feel urgent about finding a property so I can come clean to Jim, but I also want as much money as possible when I do so I can buy it outright… so I'm continuing to work on my ebooks. Now that I've spoken with these realtors, I want to let my property search take the back burner for a bit and just focus on work. But it's hard to do that knowing that my marriage is in real jeopardy, and feeling like finding the right property is the criteria I have to meet before I can talk to Jim.

Maybe I should try to find some other way to work through this with him. The last thing I want is to let things get so out of hand that I don't have a marriage to save by the time I find a property and am ready to explain myself to him.

Friday, February 13, 2015

Friday the 13th. That seems like an appropriate day for what happened today.

I finally got Jim to sit down with me for a few minutes. It turns out that he's been as concerned about our marriage as I've been, so he took steps on his own… to schedule us for marriage counseling. Today was our first meeting with the counselor.

I've got to say, it was completely weird. He floored me when he told me that he was concerned about our marriage, too, and that he wanted to try something to save things. I didn't realize he felt things were quite that dire, and I was a little shocked that he'd go ahead and schedule us for counseling without even talking to me about it. But I had to admit that it seemed like a good idea to talk to someone - maybe a counselor could help us work through things even though I'm not yet ready to admit to Jim what I've been spending so much time and effort on. So I didn't argue - I just showed up at the place and time he said.

I didn't really know what to expect. Jim came straight from work, and I came from home, so we both just… arrived there, separately. I guess that's about where our marriage is right now, anyway.

The office is near the Cambridge/Arlington border, on the edge of town near Mystic Valley Parkway. The building itself is a large multi-story home that has been converted into offices. I guess our counselor rents an office in the building. His name is on the list of providers, with about a dozen other people, and I caught myself wondering whether there are actually that many offices, or if they share space and have to schedule opposite one another.

Clearly I had some time to kill.

There wasn't really a waiting room, as such. The guy's office was a single room, and there were a couple of chairs in the hallway outside the office. Jim and I sat there, not talking, and a minute before our session was supposed to start, the door opened and a couple filed out. The therapist asked us to wait a moment while he finished up some paperwork, and then he called us into his office.

The office itself was a surprisingly soothing space. The guy is apparently into Eastern religions, as there was a Buddha and a few other things I recognized from my Eastern religion studies way back when. There were paper window treatments that felt kind of Japanese, and the walls were painted cheerful, but muted colors - one wall was a soothing peach, and another was lavender. He had a simple desk, but the desk was facing the wall instead of sitting in the middle of the room. He led us in and asked us to take a seat, and then he sat opposite us, but without any imposing furniture in between.

He asked us what we hoped to accomplish, and Jim and I just stared at each other a moment, like we were each waiting for the other to speak. And then we both started talking at once. And then we both motioned for the other to continue. It would have been comical if we hadn't been there for such a grim reason. It reminded me of how in sync we used to be, and so I spoke up, saying that we just wanted to get our marriage back on track. Jim nodded, and he looked a little relieved. I think he might have been worried that I didn't want that, or that I didn't realize how seriously out of whack things had gotten. I think it was nice for both of us to know we were on the same page, at least, in that.

Then the therapist had us talk a little about why we each thought we were there, and what it meant to each of us to "get our marriage back on track." No surprises. Jim said the stuff he's been saying to me for months now - how he felt I was drifting away and getting more distant, how I'd started neglecting friendships and activities I used to love, and how I was beginning to neglect our son. I agreed that a distance had grown between Jim and me, and that I had been busy with work and had neglected some friendships and activities I used to love, but that I was in no way neglecting our son - except for the incident where I forgot to pick him up, which I took full responsibility for. It took a surprising amount of time just for us to get through that, and for each of us to say what we thought it meant to get our marriage "back on track" - and for the therapist to tell us about how the process would work and what we could expect.

And then it was over.

Just like that.

The therapist gave us "homework" we have to do, and we'll be meeting at the same time next week.

So that's that. My husband and I are in couples counseling.

Things have definitely gone off the rails.

Saturday, February 14, 2015

Valentine's Day.

It was Jim's turn to plan Valentine's Day this year, but I didn't really have high hopes since things are in such a rocky place with our marriage.

So what did I do? I did what any self-respecting wife and mom would do when things are in dire straights.

I got a dog.

Jim slept late today, and I wanted to give him the chance to do it since he's been so upset and stressed lately. Hopefully a good night of sleep will put him in a better mood. So I packed up Ben and took him out for a special Valentine's Day breakfast, just me and my little man - and then we started puppy shopping. Surprise!

Needless to say, Ben was thrilled. He's been begging for a puppy ever since Levi got one a few years ago, but Jim and I have always put him off. As a mom working from home, I worried that dealing with a puppy on top of Ben, work and taking care of the house would just be too much for me. Ok, and yeah, I'll admit it - I wasn't thrilled about fur and dirt and who-knows-what all over the house.

But now Ben is a little older, so he's easier to manage. He can even help take care of the puppy, so it'll be a good exercise for him to learn a little about responsibility and how to care for a living thing. I was thinking about getting him a puppy for his birthday in April, anyway - doing it now just gives me a chance to surprise Jim for Valentine's Day, and hopefully give us something to love together and help get our marriage back on track.

We stopped at an animal shelter, but they told me they couldn't let me adopt a dog without all the adults in the household being present. Something about a dog being a big responsibility, and everyone having to be onboard because it's such a big commitment.

Ok, maybe that makes a little bit of sense, but I wasn't going to let their rules ruin my surprise!

I tried a few other animal shelters, and it turns out they all seem to have that rule. Bah. So much for my virtuous intent of saving a poor wittle rescue puppy's life on top of bringing home a cute little bundle of joy.

It has to be today. I have to surprise Jim, and now I've got Ben involved in the puppy hunt, so there's no way we can go home without one.

So I took Ben to the park to let him play and work off a little excitement (and some of the sugar he ate at breakfast!) while I research where to find a puppy.

It turns out, buying a puppy at a pet store isn't a good idea. I didn't know this, but most of the puppies at puppy stores come from what they call "puppy mills" - places where dogs are kept in tiny cages and basically they only get to interact with one another in order to breed. What the what? Not only are the conditions that these poor things live in downright inhumane, but there's also a high risk of the dogs having health problems, and behavioral issues, so I don't want to go anywhere near that can of worms.

Luckily, there are still a few irresponsible pet owners around whose dogs get knocked up and then they have an unexpected litter on their hands. I made some calls, and found one woman who would let me come by today and check out the puppies, and potentially take one if we like them. Apparently the mom is an English Springer Spaniel (AKC, even!) and the dad is a Border Collie, which would make it a medium-sized dog when fully grown, and smarter than average. Should have a good temperament, although if it inherited too much of its dad, it might try to herd Ben from time to time.

Well, that's fine - I could probably use a little help in that department, anyway!

So once I rounded up Ben (see, I could have totally used a herding dog already!) we went to take a look at the puppies. Maybe I should have realized that was all it would take, but once we saw them, there's no way Ben was going to leave without one. He instantly fell in love with all six, and begged for all of them. Once we made it through that little tiff, he settled on the biggest, bossiest female.

Here's where I had a little chat with the owner. She told me that males are usually a little more compliant and willing to let you run the show, but females can be headstrong and bossy. And the one Ben loved was the most headstrong and bossiest one in the litter. But there was no convincing him to take one of the boys, no matter how hard I tried - he HAD to have the boss bitch.

Why do I have a feeling that's gonna cause problems down the road?

I paid the lady a little something - way less than a pet store, might I add, and even a little bit less than a shelter - and then Ben and I took our new little bundle of joy to the local Petsmart to buy a bunch of puppy stuff.

It's a good thing I've been making so much money with my work lately, because man I had no idea how expensive a new puppy would be! I was grateful that I was driving the Outback, so I had room for everything, and I even managed to convince Ben to let the puppy ride in her new crate in the back instead of carrying her in his lap. He was dying to give her a name, but I insisted we had to let dad have the honors, since he hadn't been with us to pick her out or do the puppy shopping.

And then we headed home.

By then, it was the middle of the afternoon, and Jim had apparently started to worry about where we'd vanished to for so long. But when he saw us come in the door, his worry crinkle smoothed out into the flat, harsh planes his face becomes when he's angry.

"What have you done?" he hissed at me, giving me a significant look above Ben's happily puppy-turned face.

I spoke loud enough for Ben to hear. "We got a puppy! Ben's been wanting one for years, and I thought now might be a good time to bring a little bundle of love into our happy family. Happy Valentine's Day!" I waggled my eyebrows at him, and he just sighed and shook his head.

So he wasn't quite as happy as I'd hoped he would have been, but maybe he'll come around to the idea?

The rest of the day passed in a blur. I was expecting puppies to be a lot of work, but my God - I might have underestimated the whole thing.

On the bright side, Ben spent hours playing with her in between rounds of napping - which tired them both out, and they were absolutely adorable when they passed out together. I think they'll be fast friends.

When we pressed Jim to come up with a name, he settled on Lita, "for Lita Ford, the singer." I thought it was a little obscure, and of course Ben had no idea what the name was from, but at least Jim participated. She seems like a sweet girl - I think she'll grow on him.

Monday, February 16, 2015

My God. How can such a small puppy produce so much pee?

Where does she store it all? And how does she generate it so quickly?

Friday, February 20, 2015

What a week. I'm exhausted. I feel like I've been through the wringer. And there's no sign of it getting any better any time soon.

First of all, new puppy? WAY more work than I'd been prepared to imagine.

I've gotten maybe half as much work done this week - maybe - because I've been running around cleaning up after her, taking her out, and dealing with her myriad demands. And what I did not realize - she's too young to sleep through the night without getting up to tinkle. So guess who gets to wake up a zillion times a night to walk her? It was my idea, Jim pointed out, and I brought her home without even checking with him.

Guess who's still in the doghouse?

I didn't realize how bad it was, though, until we got to our marriage counseling session today. Instead of going over our homework (some writing we'd been asked to do around our partner and our marriage) we spent the entire time arguing about bringing home the puppy. Jim was adamant that it was a sign of how things have gone so badly wrong in our marriage. The fact that I'd make such a major decision without him, particularly when we're having problems, really seemed to piss him off.

I tried to explain why I did it. How I thought it would actually bring us closer together. That pissed him off, too.

I might have slipped a little, though, when I yelled that I didn't ask him because I knew he'd say no. I didn't actually *know* he'd say no - I just suspected - but I thought he'd love the puppy after I brought her home, and love how happy it made our son. I didn't think of it as intentionally going behind his back and subverting his authority - and failing to respect him - but apparently that's how he sees it.

Maybe things are worse than I realized in our marriage.

Anyway, I, for one, left the session feeling really shitty. We basically haven't spoken to one another the rest of the day. In the session, I offered to take the dog back, but we both know we can't do that at this point - even if the woman would take the puppy back, Ben would be heartbroken to lose her and wouldn't understand why we did it. So we can't.

Maybe I screwed up a little. But I did it to help our marriage - not to hurt Jim. And Ben really does seem to love her. So it's not all bad, right?

Thursday, February 26, 2015

It's kind of miserable in our house right now. But at least Ben is so pre-occupied with Lita that he doesn't seem to notice anything is off with his dad and me.

Jim basically hasn't been talking to me all week. He'll make some nice-nice small talk at mealtimes (when he's around - he's been staying late at work a lot and he even didn't come home a few nights - I assume he's staying at Ari's) but only when Ben is around. He hasn't said two words to me in private.

I really don't know how we're supposed to fix our marriage when we can't even talk to each other.

Anyway, the reason I'm writing today is because the real estate guy called me back. He found a property that fits my criteria up in Vermont. It's not listed through a traditional real estate firm - some woman is selling it privately - but I told him I'd pay him a finder's fee if he hears about anything non-traditional, so he's kept his ears open and called me about it.

It sounds kind of perfect. It's fifteen acres, and it's a "farmette" - which I guess means it's a small, working farm. It even has a cute little farm stand building! It has a pretty sizable barn where I could store equipment and potentially vehicles, and it's got 4 bedrooms and 2 baths. It has its own well, a small creek and a little pond for water, it has its own sewage field, and while its power is not currently off the grid, it sounds like it would be pretty easy to set something up. And it's only $125,000. Since that's only half my budget, it would leave me the same again to make it fully operational off-grid (if I borrow some from our retirement fund). Apparently it's such a steal because it's on the edge of a very small town called Island Pond, Vermont - about twenty miles from the Canadian border.

In the middle of nowhere? Check. Plenty of space to grow my own food? Double check - plus it's already set up for that. I'll have to run some simulations, (can you believe there are websites where you can run disaster simulations?) but I think it would be pretty well set up in the event of pretty much any major disaster - well inland and above sea level for rising oceans, far enough from major military targets that I wouldn't worry too much about military action, and it's in a hilly area with mountain views, which means it's probably got a good field of vision and may even be geographically defensible. The only downside is the fact that it has a small farm stand, which means the locals must know it can grow food - so if there's some kind of food shortage or isolating event, I might have to fend off the locals.

At the very least, though, it's worth going to look at it.

So that's what I'll do. I can't go tomorrow, because we have marriage counseling, but I can make an appointment to see it on Monday.

Excited about something for the first time in a while!

    I'm really learning to hate marriage counseling.

March 2015

Monday, March 2, 2015

ZOMG I love it! The property in Vermont really is perfect. So perfect that I made an offer on-the-spot. Cash.

The woman who listed it accepted the offer. I'll pay $115,000, cash, pending the results of an inspection.

I may be excited, but I'm not an idiot.

Tuesday, March 3, 2015

I forgot to mention, but Lita is in training. I saw pretty quickly that I'm not going to be able to handle this dog on my own. I need a professional to help me give her some basic manners. Fortunately, she's great with Ben, but she's kind of protective whenever we go out - apparently because she thinks she's the boss and has to take care of our family single-handedly. The training is supposed to help her realize that I'm the boss, and she doesn't have to be the one in charge.

Realistically, it's kind of adorable when a five-month-old puppy is trying to protect my son from strangers.

But Jim keeps pointing out that she won't be a five-month-old puppy forever, and I need to get ahead of this thing before she's too big to control.

She's got a good temperament, though - I think we lucked out. She's very sweet with our family, and when Ben isn't with us, she's pretty friendly to strangers. Especially when those strangers are bearing treats.

Ben is actually kind of digging the training, too. He's helping me teach her to sit, lie down and shake. The goal is to teach her to sit when greeting strangers, go to her mat at home when people come over so she's not barking at them like a fuzzy little demon when they show up at our door, and go to her crate - voluntarily - at night or for relaxation during the day.

We're making progress.

Plus, the potty training is really starting to come along.

I know it has only been a few weeks, but maybe getting a smart puppy wasn't the most horrible thing in the world.

Friday, March 6, 2015

Getting a smart puppy was, in fact, the most horrible thing in the world.

I always laughed at the "my dog ate my homework" excuse. I guess I assumed it was just something kids said in order to get out of doing their work.

Nope, turns out that at least in some cases, it's completely true.

My dog ate my… work?

My trainer tells me that when a smart dog doesn't have enough to do, it makes its own entertainment.

Either that, or our pooch was teething… or maybe she just chews out of boredom… or maybe she's mad at me for bringing her into a household full of passive-aggressive adults who won't talk to each other and where at least fifty percent of the adults weren't onboard with her being here.

Whatever the reason, she ate my laptop.

For reals. My dog ate my laptop.

Fortunately, although I haven't had a computer crash in maybe a decade, I'm kinda paranoid about backing up. We have a Time Capsule for hourly laptop backups, and I do a daily offsite backup in case something happens to the Time Capsule or our house. So the dog eating my laptop hasn't really cost me too much in the way of work.

But it did cost me over $2,000 to buy a new MacBook Pro and AppleCare.

And of course, another screaming match with my husband. Because I definitely put the dog up to it just for attention.

Or something.

Wednesday, March 11, 2015

My offer on the property was accepted! As soon as we close, I'll finally own our bug-out property and I can tell Jim what I've been working on all this time - and fix my marriage!

I had a guy do the inspection on kind of a rush basis. I paid extra because I'm eager to get this done. Everything checks out, structurally - and I found out it's only going to take around $40,000 to $50,000 to buy all the equipment to set up the property for off-grid living. Even if you assume cost overruns, that should be well within my budget - and leave plenty leftover to buy farming equipment, and even a good amount of supplies to beef up my prepper stockpile.

Which, let's face it, is already pretty badass.

I haven't really been writing about it, but as my income has gone up, I've been throwing it entirely into paying off a few bills and savings. Without mentioning it to Jim. So he's been making the same contributions to household expenses as usual, but I've paid off some bills, so our expenses are lower than usual. So I've been using the extra money to stockpile supplies.

Of course, I had to rent a storage unit to do it, because I already filled up the basement closet (he never goes in there anyway) and I have the suspicion he wouldn't quite approve of the amount of stuff I've been buying up.

But if something goes south, he'll thank me!

Anyway, all the space on the new property will give me plenty of room to store my preps. And since I'm paying cash for the property, we won't have any expenses after I set up the off-the-grid equipment, so I can spend my entire income on preps.

Jim is going to be so impressed once he sees everything I've been working toward. I can't wait until I can show him and get our marriage back on track.

I've requested a fast closing so I can start work on the property, and the seller is onboard with that since I'm paying cash - she wants the money and wants to get out of there since she lost her husband last summer - so we should be able to close by the end of the month.

So close to getting everything together!

Wednesday, March 18, 2015

Everything's coming up Della!

The past week has been really good.

Dog training with Lita is going really well. It's been a few weeks since she had a potty accident in the house. After The Great Laptop Incident of 2015, I puppy-proofed the house so everything important is out of her reach. Ben still leaves stuff lying around every now and again, and occasionally the dog eats it - but I tell him that's what he gets for leaving stuff out where Lita can chew it. Hopefully it'll teach him a lesson in responsibility.

He's doing great about playing with her every morning and every afternoon after school, to help her burn off some of her puppy energy. And he always takes her out afterward, ever since she peed in his shoe. It turns out, Levi loves her, so now he's always finding excuses to come over and hang out here with Ben - which means that when Jim comes home from work, the house is full of laughter and love and playing children and happy doggy. I think this is definitely going to help soften him toward the idea of having another child. It's not too late for me, and I think I'd really love to have another kid. Maybe a daughter, this time.

My ebooks are selling really well. Since getting the puppy last month, my productivity is going down. Right now, I'm on track to do a new ebook every month to six weeks, where before it was every two to four weeks, but as long as I keep cranking them out, they're having a cumulative effect, and I get a boost in sales every time I publish a new one.

And the best thing is, I'm researching stuff I really want to know about, and writing these ebooks based on my research and interest. So people are benefiting from the thorough research I'm doing, but I'm learning about subjects I really care about anyway - I'd do the research even if I wasn't selling the ebooks. So basically, I'm getting paid to learn how to take care of my family in a crisis.

Best. Job. Ever.

If I'd had any idea I could turn my writing chops into something like this, I would have done it years ago. Way better than all the random stuff I used to write about for my clients.

The only downer is that Jim still seems upset with me. We're still going to marriage counseling, but I don't think he's forgiven me for getting the dog, and it feels like he's just going through the motions in counseling. He barely talks to me outside of sessions, except stuff to do with Ben.

Can't wait until I close on the house in Vermont and can finally share my secret with him. Then everything will be fixed, and my family will be better than ever.

Monday, March 23, 2015

I close on the property on Thursday. Because I'm doing all this secretly, and paying cash, it'll be just my name on the closing docs. I couldn't find any way to get Jim listed without having him there, and I want to surprise him. But I can amend the deed once I tell him about it, so I think he won't mind too much once he understands the point of it.

Now I'm trying to decide when to tell him, and how to tell him. Part of me wants to take him and Ben up there this weekend to show them our awesome new bug-out property. But another part of me wants to wait until the work is all done, so it's fully off the grid - and I get some furniture and stuff in there - so we can actually stay up there if we want.

I've got a few days to think about it. But maybe it would be easier to get work done before they know about it. I'll see about finding contractors and getting prices and timeframes, and maybe that'll help me decide.

Well, apparently all is not quite well in Connorland. Got a call from school today - Ben had a full-on meltdown. Like, call the parents in and have a conference meltdown. Like, he's a short hair away from getting suspended meltdown. I think I've headed that off at the pass, but man - he's never been in this kind of trouble before.

I got the call. Jim couldn't get out of work, even though the school wanted both of us there, so I went by myself. Ben was sitting outside the principal's office, looking pouty. He didn't even try to offer me an excuse, so I guess that was my first sign it was serious. (Well, aside from the call.)

When I got into the office, there was already another set of parents waiting. The principal sat at her desk, and Ben's teacher was there, too. So it was serious enough that they dragged the teacher out of class, and there was another kid involved.

The principal asked me to sit down and then proceeded to tell me about how my son had flat-out attacked another boy. Apparently it all started as a dispute over crayons. Ben wanted the colors that the other kid was using, and he wasn't done with them yet so he didn't give them up. (Personally, I think they're a little old for this - I thought Ben graduated from crayons a few years ago - but maybe they were doing some sort of art project?)

When the other kid wouldn't give them up, Ben then proceeded to push the poor kid out of his chair and onto the floor, grab up one of the colors he wanted, and scribble all over the other kid's project. Then, when the teacher came in their direction, Ben ripped up the paper and threw the pieces at the other kid, who was sitting on the floor, crying.

Honestly, I'm not sure how serious this sort of thing is. Because Ben's never been in this kind of trouble before, I haven't really looked into it. He's so good at cooperating with other kids and sharing. Karate helps with that, I think, and he's always been good with his friends at playgroup and when he has other kids over. So this is coming completely out of left field.

The teacher then went on to say that Ben had been acting out in class for a while now. Apparently he's been giving her attitude, and arguing with the other kids. But he hasn't been bringing his conduct reports home for me to sign, and I haven't heard anything from the teacher, so I had no idea.

I guess maybe I slipped a little in not noticing that the conduct reports had stopped coming. But honestly, I've been so busy with everything, it didn't even occur to me they were missing. And Jim never deals with them, so of course he wasn't there to back me up.

Well, I explained to them that I hadn't seen any sign of this behavior at home. I told them about the new puppy, and how much Ben loves her and is involved in her training and care. And how his friend Levi has been spending extra time over, and Ben's been fine with him. I didn't go so far as to say the problem was with the other kid, but I talked about how he's never had a problem sharing before and maybe he was just having an off day. Maybe he hadn't gotten enough sleep or eaten enough at breakfast. Although of course I apologized to the other parents, and said we would definitely have a talk with him at home to make sure he understood that kind of behavior wasn't acceptable, and that he owed their son an apology.

The principal then asked the other parents to leave the room. After they were gone, she told me that this kind of behavior usually indicates that something is happening to stress the child out. Like something in his life is making him feel uncomfortable, unsafe or unsettled. And then she had the nerve to ask if anything was going on at home! I think she was trying to play the "It's just women here" card with me - her and the teacher looking at me sympathetically and telling me it was a safe space and I could tell them if something was happening.

I could not believe they went there. Of course I told them that Ben and I are perfectly happy and safe at home with Jim and the new puppy. They kept probing, and I hated the implication that we might be in a domestic abuse situation, so I finally admitted that Jim and I had been going to marriage counseling to work through a few division of responsibility issues. Nothing remotely related to domestic abuse. They gave each other this knowing look and gave me all kinds of sympathy, and I just wanted to punch them. I really did. I've never felt so violent toward another human being as I felt in that office, with their smug faces judging my family and thinking the worst just because my son had a (first) minor temper tantrum at school.

At least they decided to go easy after I admitted that, and agreed not to suspend him. But I get the impression they won't be so easy on him a second time around - and they said they were going to write up the incident and have it in his record!

I don't really know what to think right now. I'm still torn between outrage at the teacher and principal, being annoyed with Ben for behaving so badly, and being upset with myself and feeling like I've failed him as a mother. None of these are pleasant feelings.

I talked with Ben about it at length after I brought him home. I still need to talk with Jim about what happened. I gave him a basic summary, but we probably need to talk about how our conflict is making Ben uncomfortable. I just don't know when to find the time - as soon as Ben went to bed, Jim got sucked into some work thing and still hasn't come to bed. I think he might still be avoiding me.

Thursday, March 26, 2015

Closing day! I am now the proud owner of a nice little bug-out property in Vermont! Woohoo!

After yesterday's drama with Ben at school, I was a little apprehensive about today going smoothly. I kept worrying that I'd get another call from school, or that something would fall through with the closing - just SOMETHING would go wrong. But nothing did!

As soon as I get Ben off to school in the morning, I'm heading up to the house. I've got a couple of contractors lined up to visit tomorrow, because I want to start some of the work on the property. I'm having Levi's parents take the kids after school, and I guess I'll just bring the dog with me. I'll probably be home late and I can't leave her at home all day, so I hope she'll be good in the car and while I'm talking with the contractors.

The keys to the house are burning a hole in my pocket. I want to head up there now, but I didn't make any arrangements for Ben and it's too late in the day to get home before he does. So I guess I'll do some more research on solar systems and off-grid utilities so I can communicate what I want more clearly to the contractors.

Friday, March 27, 2015

Contractors! Contractors are the worst. One guy actually showed up on time, but he was completely useless. He didn't seem to understand what I wanted at all, and he kept trying to tell me I need to do stuff I have no intention of touching. Whatever.

The next guy showed up an hour late, but at least he understood what I was trying to say. I didn't like the way he was looking at me or the house, though. I need to get a security system up and running ASAP. I'll work on that next week.

The third guy was ridiculously late - I was about to have to leave to get home when he arrived. However, he was great with Lita, and he actually seemed into the off-the-grid projects I want to do. In fact, he even made some suggestions of his own - different placement for the solar panels, different ways to run the wiring, stuff we'd need to do electrically to get the house powered off solar, and some thoughts on making the plumbing completely self-sufficient. Also, some ideas for making the house more energy efficient to heat and cool, and ideas for heating in the winter. (Solar collector, for one thing - I never thought of something like that - changing out some windows, adding some insulation in a few areas, etc. And of course, a wood-burning stove, which apparently is much more efficient than a fireplace. I didn't know about that.)

Just based on how helpful he was, I'll probably end up hiring him, even if he was ridiculously late. He also claims to know a good electrician who can help with the solar wiring, and he suggested some vendors who might be able to give me a deal on the equipment. I'd already done some research on that myself - I knew one of the names - but he had two others that I need to contact. I just hope his quote is reasonable, but even if it's not, I have a sneaking suspicion I'll pay it just to get him involved in the project.

Well. Anyway, it's late - I'm actually into the wee hours of Saturday AM, and of course Jim has gone to bed without waiting for me. Off to join him. Maybe we can spend some time together this weekend and improve things a bit.

Saturday, March 28, 2015

Ugh. We rescheduled yesterday's marriage counseling for today, since I wasn't around yesterday, and that might not have been the best idea. At least on Friday, Jim goes back to work and I have Ben and my own work to distract me after counseling is over, and things are usually a little better by the time we meet up again in the evening. But today, we went straight from breakfast to dropping Ben off at Levi's to counseling - and then we had no more Ben, but we were stuck together for the rest of the day. So our marriage counseling session sorta spilled over into the rest of our day, and it has not been a good day.

I talked about what happened with Ben at school, and how I'm concerned that our difficulties are affecting him. I was hoping the therapist would have some productive ideas of how to deal with it. But I hadn't actually had a chance to talk to Jim about any of that stuff yet, because he was avoiding me on Wednesday and Thursday, and he went to bed early last night. So it was the first time he was hearing about it, and he was NOT happy. He kept trying to turn it around on me. Saying that our marriage problems are MY fault, and if I was a better mom to Ben he wouldn't be stressed out, or picking up on our difficulties - or we wouldn't be having issues at all…

Ok, that's fair, I'll take the blame for some of it. I have been keeping secrets (for a good reason!) and I did get a little too busy and mess up on a few things. But I'm still one hundred percent committed to my marriage, and I still love Jim, and I'm not the one who's shutting down and pushing the other person away. That's all him. He talks to me at marriage counseling, and he pretends to be ok when Ben is around, but when it's just the two of us, he barely says two words to me. He's always going off to do work stuff, or going to bed early, or finding some excuse to not actually interact with me. It's like he can't or won't forgive me. Honestly, I'm not really sure why he's even doing marriage counseling if he won't actually try to make things right between us.

Ugh. I can't believe I just typed that. I can't believe I'm thinking that. I love my husband. I know he loves me. Or he used to, anyway. I can't believe I'm thinking about how he might be having second thoughts about our marriage, or just not willing to work things out with me.

Alright. Enough. No more typing today, because if I keep going, I'm going to overthink this and get all worried and stressed out about something that is probably nothing…

Sunday, March 29, 2015

Thank God for Ben. I love that kid so much. When he came home this afternoon, everything was fine again. It didn't matter that Jim and I barely spoke last night or this morning. It didn't feel like a cloud of doom was hanging over the house anymore. It just felt like home.

Tuesday, March 31, 2015

I've been vetting vendors for the solar system supplies, and I think I'm actually going to go with one of the companies that Charlie recommended. (He's the contractor I'm going to hire. I don't care what he asks. I've been trading emails and occasional texts with him as I look at various options for the house, and he's so knowledgeable and already invested in the project. I'm sure he'll be worth every penny.)

I'm just running some numbers on what the house has used historically, and what I think I can get away with by swapping out energy-efficient appliances and making the house a little more energy efficient in general, so I can decide how much solar power I'm going to need. I could probably let Charlie do all the work and figure out what to order... but I really want to know what I've got and how everything works so that I can service the system myself. After all, when the shit hits the fan, Charlie won't be around - I'm going to have to be able to take care of everything in the house on my own. So I'm not going to leave it up to someone else to put the system together. I may even try to stay up there while the work is going on so I can see what he's doing and learn a few things about how the system works. It'll be nice to know in practice versus in theory.

Jim's still being weird. The weekend was awkward and uncomfortable. I need to never have a marriage counseling session on a Saturday again. I also need to talk to him about what he's hoping to get out of these sessions, because I'm just not sure anymore that he actually wants to save our marriage. As much as I've told myself not to overthink it, I can't help thinking about it. And I just don't see any progress happening on his side.

So I've gotta find time to talk to him. On top of being a mom time, and researching stuff for the house time, and oh, yeah, by the way, writing more ebooks and dealing with my business...

April 2015

Friday, April 3, 2015

Ok, things with Jim are… weird. I wanted to get back to a better place with him, so I talked in therapy today about how I felt like he wasn't really trying. I said I was concerned that he was just going through the motions, and talked about how he's been avoiding me… and he listened. He said he heard me. And then he took me out to dinner! We dropped Ben off with Levi and we just went out together and sat and had food and talked, just like a regular couple. Like we used to.

And then we went back home, and he actually poured us wine and lit candles and put on music. I can't remember the last time he's done that. We haven't really made love… well, I can't remember the last time we did that, either, actually. But when we do, as a couple that's been together forever and has a son and has to steal moments together between being tired and work and everything… romance is very much an afterthought. But he actually put in the effort.

On the one hand, I had a wonderful evening. It reminded me of what we used to have.

On the other hand, it was… weird. We may have had that before, but we're not really there now. I was just thinking we need to talk more, and really honestly work at our relationship. I wasn't really suggesting we try to go back to the way it was before and skip through all the interim stuff.

It felt awkward. Kind of like that first time you have sex with someone, and you don't really know the other person's moves or what they like. But we've been together forever, so we're way past that point. Or at least, I thought we were.

Well, whatever. It's nice to have him trying again. Ben is spending the night at Levi's, but maybe tomorrow we can go do something as a family. And his birthday is coming up soon, so I'll bring it up with Jim and see what we want to do this year. Maybe I'll tap one of the other moms and see what the kids are doing right now.

Monday, April 6, 2015

What a great weekend. My God, I can't remember the last time we had such a good weekend together. We had a blast with the kiddo (and Levi on Sunday - he came to us because he wanted to play with Lita)… and the fun continued after Ben was asleep. It might have been weird on Friday, but we seem to have gotten our groove back. Wow. What a nice change. I'm feeling more relaxed and easygoing than I have in… I can't remember how long.

Checked with one of the other moms about party ideas, and she said the big thing right now is some indoor water park in a hotel in Danvers. I looked into it - Coco Key - and it turns out we can rent a 'cabana' - their version of a private room - and have food delivered, and they've got the waterpark and an arcade, so I think it'll be a big hit. When I brought it up with Jim this evening, he was totally into the idea and seemed surprised but happy that I'd done the footwork. I was a little offended by that part, actually. I know I've dropped the ball once or twice in the past six months, but I'm not completely checked out. Ben is my son, and I love him dearly, and I hate disappointing him. It's not like I'd let that become a cycle.

Wednesday, April 8, 2015

It's official: Charlie is my contractor. His bid actually wasn't the highest - he came in right in the middle - but with all the help he's already been, and with all the interest and expertise he's bringing to the project, I may have to give him a bonus when it's all done. Especially as my next ebook is going to be about off-grid systems for your home, with a strong focus on solar setups - which incorporates a lot of information I've gleaned from Charlie or his electrician associate, David. Plus the company where we're buying the equipment. I think it'll be a good resource for other people who are setting up off-the-grid living situations, so hopefully it'll sell well. Maybe it'll pay his bonus!

I headed up to the house yesterday to sign the agreement with Charlie and make a few final decisions in-person at the space. Something struck me as... off, somehow. I can't put my finger on what it was, but I definitely feel like I need to get a security system up and running ASAP. I can go with basic ADT for now, but I want some specialty stuff setup for when SHTF. I want to be able to see anyone who's coming onto my property, have some self-defense options in place, and have some evacuation options in case I can't defend us. Because we never know what kind of threat we might be up against, and I'm not going to leave myself vulnerable to unfriendlies after working so hard to get everything set up.

I might ask Charlie if he wants to stay out there while he's working. It's a pretty nice place - he's admired it while we've been talking shop - and I'd feel better knowing that someone is there in case someone comes snooping around.

In mom news, I've booked the water park place for Ben's birthday next week. Jim is totally onboard, and seems really impressed with me getting things together. I told him I'm a little offended by how he's acting like it's completely out of character for me to be on top of things, when I feel like that's pretty normal for me. He admitted that he'd been losing faith in me after I dropped the ball on that stuff months ago - his holiday party, and forgetting to pick Ben up that time - and that he just feels like things are finally back on track after those mess-ups.

I'm glad he feels that way... but I kinda resent that he's been holding those things against me so much. It's not like he's perfect and has never made a mistake, but he's sure acting like my mess-ups were deal breakers while he's never had any at all. I guess now it's my turn to work on forgiving him and moving forward.

Saturday, April 11, 2015

I've got to get some time away to spend up at the house in Vermont. Next weekend is Ben's birthday party, and then maybe I'll tell Jim I need to travel for work for like a week. He can handle stuff around here - the dog can go to daycare while he's at work, and Levi's mom can help out with all the after school stuff for a few days. Actually, I'd like to bring the dog with me, but I couldn't explain that if I'm supposed to be traveling for work.

I want to be up at the Vermont house for two reasons: one, stuff will be starting to come in during the next week or two, and I want to make sure it's the right stuff; and two, I still feel like something's going on at the house, and I want to be up there. ADT got a system installed for me, and Charlie signed off on it, but he said he's been visiting the house at random times and he thinks something is going on there, too.

He said stuff is moved around sometimes, or he'll see tire tracks if it's been wet (which is pretty much all the time these days - I need to make sure there's ample storage from the solar system to get me through the rainy/snowy New England winters and springs).

Part of me wonders if it's that creepy contractor guy I didn't like when I interviewed people - the guy who was eyeing up me and the house - but if so, I don't know what he'd be doing up there. On the other hand, who else would it be? The couple who owned the house before had been there forever, and the lady never said anything about this kind of problem.

This is why I'd like to have the dog with me. She's great at hearing and noticing things I just don't. But I can't figure out an excuse to get away that would let me bring her. Unless, maybe I can sell it as a dog-friendly writer's retreat that I've won for a week... maybe as a raffle prize... hmm. I'll have to think about it.

Wednesday, April 15, 2015

Ugh. Tax day.

Just kidding! I got my taxes done early this year, so I breezed right through today without an ounce of stress. It's a nice change from the days of "Oh shit! Need to file an extension because I don't have all my paperwork together!" Or, the even more dreaded, "Oh shit! I can't afford to pay what I owe as a self-employed person." I really don't miss those days.

That being said, I think my taxes are going to be a little more complicated next year. What with buying the Vermont house, and with my ebooks bringing in so much money now, my tax situation will have changed quite substantially. In fact, I probably should be withholding more than I am right now - I'm definitely not in the same tax bracket anymore. Maybe I should wait a few weeks for the tax frenzy to die down, and then work on finding a good accountant who can help me out.

In the meantime, I'm just happy to be making enough to fund all the work on the Vermont house. One of the prepper sites picked up one of my ebooks, and I've been getting a LOT of hits since then - and a lot of sales. I've gotten a few requests for more information about specific topics, and some interview requests, and a ton of feedback - most of it good - so I guess people are happy with what I've been doing. I bet they'd be chuffed to know that their support is paying for my own bug-out space. But I'm not ready to talk about that until I've told Jim - I wouldn't want something to get back to him before I'm ready to reveal it.

Friday, April 17, 2015

Ben's birthday party is tomorrow! We're actually all set. He's got 10 of his friends coming (plus their parents) so I've reserved three cabanas at the water park, and I've got a ton of food options set up. The dog's going to daycare, I pick up the cake in the morning, Ben's present is wrapped and waiting in my closet, and we are all ready for an awesome afternoon. I've already got a bag packed with plates and serving things for the cake, although I shouldn't have to provide them because the venue should be taking care of that. But you never know, and I like to be prepared. I've also beefed up my mom bag, with extra first aid supplies, Kleenex and emergency foods that should see us through.

Being a mom is a lot like being a prepper. It's all about being prepared for the most common crises, with enough extra supplies to help you handle pretty much anything that might come your way.

Although I probably should carry some peanut-free granola bars in case I ever have to feed a kid with a peanut allergy. It's always a toss-up whether another parent is horrified when they see me feeding my son peanuts, or whether they high five me for refusing to bow down to the establishment.

Maybe I need to hang around with different parents.

Anyway, we're ready. Bring on the party!

Saturday, April 18, 2015

Party was a success! And by "success," I mean that the only child meltdowns that occurred did not involve my son, and weren't a result of my failure to do anything. It's not *my* fault that one of the kids freaked out when his dad wouldn't give him any more quarters for the arcade, and had to leave the party because he couldn't calm himself down. (I had plenty of extra quarters. But it was his dad's call when the poor tyke was done, so I couldn't help with my preparedness in this case.) And there was a minor issue when one of the kids was jealous over one of the gifts that Ben had gotten - I still don't know which one - and had a tantrum, so his mom had to take him outside for a time out while the rest of us enjoyed the cake.

Man, that cake was good! So glad I found that little bakery.

Ben was having Levi sleep over for his birthday, and those two were barely able to keep it together through dinner. By the time we settled them down with a movie after they ate, they were out like a light. Jim and I had a really pleasant evening after they went down, actually.

It still feels a little weird that things are so good between us right now. I hate that it feels weird. I want this to be the normal state of things, but it's all been so strained between us for the past few months that I forgot what it felt like to have a husband who actually wanted to spend time with you, didn't avoid you in bed, and was generally pleasant to be around. I do like it, but… it's weird.

I guess I'm waiting for the other shoe to fall. It all started so suddenly, and it felt like no matter what I did I couldn't make a difference - I just couldn't get through to him and he wasn't forgiving me. And now it's all ended just as abruptly. We're still working on stuff in therapy, but honestly it feels like we don't even need it anymore. And I don't trust that at all.

Monday, April 20, 2015

Made it up to the house in Vermont. I went with the "won a raffle for a week-long writer's retreat" idea so I could bring Lita, and Jim didn't bat an eyelash. I've gotta say, now that I'm up here and it's dark, I'm glad to have her with me.

I really love the house. I hope Jim and Ben love it as much as I do, but I don't see how they couldn't. It's just wonderful here. Everything feels so warm and inviting and cozy. There's not a ton of stuff I need to do to the inside - we're swapping out the appliances for more energy-efficient versions, and we're going to change a few of the windows. As we go through that process, Charlie is going to check out the walls and see whether any of them would benefit from extra insulation. But this place seems really well-built and solid, so I'm hopeful we won't have to do too much and most of it will just be installing off-grid options for the systems.

Even so, now that it's dark outside, I feel... uneasy here in the house. I decided to turn off the lights in here and hang out in the dark, so if someone does come out here, they won't know there's anyone inside. That gives me a little extra security - I'll know they're there before they know I'm here. It also means I won't be a target, because no-one will know to look for me. But it does feel a little silly hanging out here in the dark. And a little lonely. Thank God for the dog.

Better shut my laptop now, because I don't want the light from the screen to give me away. But I'll be keeping my eye out.

Tuesday, April 21, 2015

OMG!!! I can hardly believe I'm writing this, but someone is really fucking around on my property! Last night, after I wrote the entry and went dark, I hung out for a while, waiting and watching. I think I dozed a little on the couch, cozy under a blanket, when a set of headlights woke me up. Headlights in the house are pretty obvious, because we're a ways off the road and behind the trees, so headlights don't usually make it back here. But damned if someone wasn't driving out here!

They drove right up, got out, and walked around the property with a flashlight. I couldn't get a clear look because of the dark, but it was only one person and I think it was a guy. I had put my car in the barn and installed a new lock on it, so it wouldn't be so obvious that someone is here right now. But he did try the barn and find the lock. So I guess it's obvious that someone has been here.

He wandered around for a while, and then went back to the cab of his truck. He sat there for a while. I settled in to watch. Eventually, he turned around and left again. I thought it was a little strange that he didn't bother the house at all, or try to look in any of the windows, but I have no idea what business he thinks he has here. It sure as Hell didn't feel like a random visit.

I didn't feel safe after that. Hell, I didn't feel safe when I first saw him pull up. I'm going to install some motion sensor lights outside today, and maybe add a few more locks to the doors. And I might ask Charlie if he has any thoughts or recommendations for me. It's early morning now - I didn't sleep well after that and was up at first light - so I've probably still got an hour or two before he gets here to start work. I wonder how quickly I can get some of the other security stuff set up - like the video surveillance on the front drive, at least?

Wednesday, April 22, 2015

I feel both good and bad about this trip up here. A lot is going on right now.

The good: stuff is finally showing up, and not only am I getting to watch Charlie install it - he's letting me help! This gives me first-hand knowledge of how things are put together, and is an excellent basis for how to fix them down the road if something goes wrong. Charlie is really great, actually - he's patient, and good at explaining what he's doing, and insightful, and funny, too. I'm glad to have met him, and I wish I had more friends like him back in Boston.

The bad: someone is definitely up to no good. I got the motion sensor lights installed yesterday, and talked to Charlie about what I saw, so he stayed with me here in the house last night. He said he wouldn't feel safe leaving me here alone if he knew someone was sniffing around out here.

It was a little weird hanging around in the dark with a semi-stranger. We chatted, and told stories, and I don't quite feel like he's a stranger anymore. More like a new friend I don't know very well yet. But it still felt weird to be sitting around alone in the dark with him.

To the point, though: sure enough, someone came snooping around out here again last night. There isn't room in the barn for Charlie's work truck and my car, so we parked it behind the barn so it would be out of sight from the drive and the house.

The person drove up the drive the same way they did on Monday night, but stopped short when the red truck he was driving hit one of the motion sensor lights. He sat in the truck, waiting, while the light shone down on him. I think he was trying to see if someone was going to come out and confront him for being somewhere he wasn't supposed to be, but we sat tight in the house so eventually he drove on past the light and stopped the truck. He got out and started walking around with the flashlight, but soon enough, he hit another one of the motion sensor lights (the one in front of the barn). He jumped back when the light came on, and stood just out of its range, but we could see that he was wearing a baseball cap and had the hood of his scruffy coat pulled up, so we couldn't identify the guy.

He stood still for a long time - until the motion sensor light turned off again - but he must have balls of steel because he didn't turn around and get back in his truck. Instead, he skirted the clearing where the house is located, giving the buildings a wide berth but walking all over the property. He went back behind the barn, and I assume he saw Charlie's truck, but he kept on going - we saw the flashlight emerge on the other side of the barn pretty quickly - so we didn't think he had time to try to screw with the truck. I guess we can't even be sure he saw it, but I don't know how he could have missed it.

He didn't come anywhere near the house - I guess he was concerned about tripping more motion sensor lights - but eventually he did turn off the flashlight and did who knows what on one side of the property. I don't know if he was trying to move through the dark - worried someone might be watching and the flashlight might give him away - or if he had something else in mind. It's impossible to guess when I have no idea what he's doing here in the first place.

Eventually, the flashlight came back on and he headed back to his truck. He got back in, and sat in the cab for a long while again. Charlie agreed it's really weird - we have no idea what the guy is doing but it's definitely strange.

Finally, he backed the truck down the long driveway again. I thought it was strange that he didn't just turn around, but Charlie pointed out that since the guy was backing away, we couldn't catch his license plate. Instead of a front number plate, he had one of the "Vermont Strong" plates that they did as a fundraiser after Irene. Charlie says those things are expired now - now you're required to use a front plate again - but apparently this guy didn't get the memo. As he backed out, he activated the motion sensor light on the driveway again, but sure enough - we couldn't get any identifying information off the pickup truck. Although maybe a red truck that's still running a "Vermont Strong" plate would be enough to locate him.

I tried calling the police today, but they said that unless the man commits a crime, they can't do anything about it. I pointed out that he's trespassing. They asked if I have any "No Trespassing" signs posted. Turns out, I have to post very specific signage to indicate that this is private property if I want to enforce trespassing. And even if I do, I pretty much have to catch him in the act - like calling the police and getting them out while he's still here. And even if that happens, the max penalty for trespassing without actually entering any of the buildings on my property is up to three months in jail, or five hundred dollars.

Somehow, getting this guy on a basic trespassing charge just doesn't seem strong enough. I don't know what he's doing out here, but I feel like he has to be up to no good. Maybe he's casing the place and intends to break in once he knows the property well enough. Or maybe he's waiting for me to move in, and finding places where he could sit and watch me, or… worse.

Oh God. This just got really creepy.

Jim called to check on how my writer's retreat is going. I want to tell him all about the weird dude and the good progress we're making here otherwise, but of course I can't say a word. It feels kind of uneasy to be keeping so much from him. It's getting to be a very heavy secret, so I don't know how much longer I want to carry on keeping him in the dark. I wanted it to be all ready for us before I show him, but the longer I don't tell him, the worse I think it feels. And potentially, the more unhappy he could be, if he decides to be upset that I kept this a secret from him.

I hope he understands why. I hope he sees that I wanted to surprise him, and that I wanted it to be all ready so it would win him over. I want him to see the great potential that this place has, just like I do.

Well, anyhow. No use borrowing trouble. I'm here for the rest of the week. Charlie says he's definitely going to stay as long as I'm here, because after seeing that guy last night, he does not trust what he's up to. So I guess I've got my first houseguest. Off to the grocery to pick up some extra stuff to feed my erstwhile guardian.

In the meantime, I need to ponder what to do about this guy snooping around my property. I don't want to let him continue unchecked while I'm gone. It's bad enough when I'm here and I can keep an eye on him, and all he's doing is walking around the place. But if he's working up to something more… I don't want to leave the place unoccupied to let him get away with… whatever.

Thursday, April 23, 2015

Last night was the best night I had in… I can't remember how long.

I am SO in trouble.

First of all, the creep did not show up last night. I don't know if the motion sensor lights scared him off, or if he's taking a break, or if he doesn't come out every night… I really have no idea what he's about, so it's impossible to predict his behavior. It worries me, though.

But what worries me more is how much I'm enjoying spending time with Charlie.

We sat in the dark again last night, waiting for the creep to show up. I left the barn unlocked and hid my car in the woods, so I was thinking maybe if he came and tried to get into the barn, I could get him on breaking and entering and not just trespassing. It carries a stiffer penalty.

So Charlie and I sat around talking, in the dark, while we waited for the guy to show up.

It was one of those amazing talks, like you have when you're young and falling in love. The kind of talk where you spend the entire night talking about everything and nothing. When you talk about your deepest fears, your biggest dreams, and the meaning of life - and feel amazingly intelligent and connected and… and deeply attracted to the other person.

I confessed to Charlie how I felt my marriage was falling apart. I didn't even realize it until the words came out, but there it was - truth. Jim and I are going through the motions, but I'm not sure either of us is trying anymore. And when you stop trying, there's no way to resurrect a broken relationship. It just ain't happening.

So the bigger question becomes: why am I not trying? Why is he not trying? Do we even *want* to save our marriage? Maybe we're just growing apart. This happens to a lot of couples. It wouldn't be the end of the world.

It's ironic. The problems that started all of these issues have stemmed from me trying to be prepared in the event that something catastrophic happens. Trying to keep my family safe - because I love them, so much - is what started driving us apart.

But maybe things were already broken before that happened. I've messed up a couple of times, but what kind of marriage can't withstand a few mistakes and an honest effort to set things right? I've been busting my ass to get Jim to forgive me, and he's just not budging. So maybe the problem is with us - not the little mishaps I've had.

I don't know what to do. I love Ben with all of my heart. My little boy is my world. And up until last night, I would have said the same thing about Jim. But now… I'm not sure.

What kind of woman can be attracted to another man if she's still in love with her husband? Is this a sign that I should give up on my marriage?

Friday, April 24, 2015

Friday. The end of my week here in Vermont. Well, I'll stay through Sunday morning, but it's the end of hanging out with Charlie while he's working on my house. He has every right to a Monday through Friday gig - no reason I should ask him to work Saturday just because I'm here and I want to learn from what he's doing. Or because I'm not sure when I'll get back up here again, and I want to enjoy every moment with him that I can.

I just keep telling myself that I may get up here during the day, once or twice, but I won't be spending any more nights until my husband is here with me. Which means no Charlie.

Sure, I might see him for an hour or two here or there if I come back up to finish up any last details, and when I sign off on the project. But no more of these endless nights in the dark - these times when we're not employer and employee but friends and… something more? Friends with potential? Is that a thing? If not, it should be.

Get ahold of yourself, woman. This may be your diary, but that doesn't give you carte blanche to ramble on endlessly while you moon over some man.

Ahem. Ok.

So today's the last day I can be here with him. I'm asking Charlie if we can focus on the solar panel install. He's run home now for a shower, but he'll be back in a few to start work. I'm supposed to be working on breakfast, but I had to steal a moment to jot a few thoughts down…

The creep didn't come back again last night. Instead, we spent most of the night chatting, with a little napping thrown in. We're both a little exhausted because of the lack of sleep. Is it so bad if we nap on the same couch, under the same blanket? I stay on my end, and he's on his end, but our legs mingle in the middle and it feels so comfortable and comforting. And yeah… maybe a little bit tingly in the tummy. I haven't had butterflies since Jim and I started dating. It's been a *long* time.

Oh. Right. Not rambling about Charlie.

Solar panel. Breakfast. I'll come back to this later. Or tomorrow.

Saturday, April 25, 2015

Well, as a writer's retreat, this has been a total fail. I've gotten absolutely no writing done on my ebooks, which isn't great because I could use the money after all this work on the house. I'm still bringing in a very comfortable income - a surprisingly comfortable income, truth be told - but all of this equipment and these energy efficient appliances and windows have been expensive. And Charlie and David, too, of course.

Charlie spent some time on Thursday on the windows. It turns out I really could use some more insulation in the walls, so he's going to spend some time tearing into things and seeing what he can do to make the whole building more energy efficient. I think he plans to work on the solar collector next week. The generators should come next week, too, so we might be just about ready to finish the solar setup.

I ended up admitting to Charlie last night that I was disappointed not to see all of the work through. I told him what a pleasure it's been watching him work and learning as he went along, and how helpful I think I'll find it when it comes to keeping the house maintained in the long run.

Well, it doesn't matter what I say, anyway. We've done so much talking that I've told him all about my prepping, and the horrible things I'm worried could bring our world crashing to a halt. He knows I want to know everything I can so I can repair stuff down the road, when SHTF and my family is left to rely on its own devices. And he's actually really cool about it. He told me he's going to start doing his own prepping. He doesn't have a place in the woods like mine, but he can put together some food and supplies, and maybe do some work on his place to keep his supplies hidden and safe. I don't know if he can afford to go all out like I am, though, and do all the off-the-grid stuff.

Anyway, Charlie was really nice when I said that stuff last night about being disappointed I can't be here for more of the work. So he's actually coming back to work today, even though it's Saturday and he should be free to do his own stuff or take time off. I'm really grateful for the chance to learn more from him before I go.

Tonight will be our last night together before I take off. I'm going home tomorrow. I can't see this happening again. Even if I came back, and stayed overnight without Jim, the creep hasn't been back in days, so Charlie probably wouldn't feel the need to stay over and look after me.

I have mixed feelings about all of this. On the one hand, I don't want to feel unsafe in my own home. Especially when it's a home I bought specifically for long-term safety and survival.

On the other hand, I've really enjoyed this time with Charlie. I know nothing can come of it, but that doesn't stop me from wanting more.

What a mess.

Don't know where to start. Last night was… well, it defied expectation. As in, it was so bizarre and surreal I could never have predicted anything that happened.

For starters, I'm still in Vermont.

I'm in the hospital, in fact.

You know who else is in the hospital? Charlie.

He saved my life.

After we kissed.

Maybe I should go back a bit.

I made dinner for us. I wanted to show my appreciation for him coming to work on a Saturday, and for all he's done this week - for staying at the house to look after me, for letting me watch him work and pester him with a million questions, and for being so invested in the project (and willing to make suggestions). I snuck out and picked up place settings and wine glasses, and served some red wine with dinner. We got very mellow and happy, and we forgot to blow out the candles right away when we finished eating. (I figured candles were a little less conspicuous than bright electrical lights, because we needed something to see our food after it got dark…)

Well, anywho. We were sitting on the couch, chatting with our wineglasses, when there was a pause… and we kissed. I don't know who started it. It wasn't anything we talked about or planned. One moment, we were just happy friends enjoying a conversation… and the next moment, we were kissing.

It was a short kiss, but oh-so-sweet and tender and full of promise. Who knows where it might have led if things hadn't turned out the way they did?

We kissed. Then we separated a few inches, gazing at each other while we tried to work out who had started it and what came next. And that's when Charlie told me he noticed the laser dot on my face

He lunged up and forward to shove me down onto the couch, out of the line of sight of the windows, and the shooter chose that precise moment to take the shot. The one bullet caught us both - it caught Charlie in the shoulder, and then me, nearly severing my subclavian artery. That's a fancy doctor term for the spot near where my clavicle and neck meet.

He took a quick moment to shove a couch pillow against my wound, telling me to "Hold it there, tight!" and then sprang into action.

I could barely parse what he was doing, he moved so quickly. He tumbled off the couch in a quasi-somersault, rolling as he came up and grabbing something from under his coat on the back of the dining room chair. He snuffed the candles quickly, and picked up the night vision monocular I'd bought a few days earlier from where we'd left it on the table.

Then he moved to one of the side windows, popping up and scanning the area quickly with the monocular before popping back down again. I watched him sprint from window to window, barely breathing, terrified I'd hear another shot ring out and see him go down. After he'd circled the house, checking all of the windows, he came back to where I waited on the couch.

He asked where I'd stashed my bandages - of course I've got ample first aid supplies, as a prepper - and I must have had enough brain to answer him, but I don't know what I said. The last thing I remember is him talking to a 911 dispatcher as he headed toward the bandages.

The next thing I remember clearly is waking up this morning, here.

There are flashes in between. Charlie, hovering over me, poking at my wound with a hemostat. Being loaded into an ambulance, and someone asking me questions. The flash of lights passing above me as I was wheeled down a hallway, presumably in the hospital. And I swear I saw someone in a face mask once, who must have been my doctor from the surgery, but I'm told I was out cold and couldn't possibly have seen any of that.

When I woke up this morning, Jim was here. He's listed as my emergency contact, and I guess someone must have notified him. He says he dropped of Ben with Levi's family - I guess it must not have been too late when everything went sideways.

He looked horrible. He had dark smudges under his eyes, and his whole face was droopy. I'd catch him looking at me with these sad eyes. And his nose was red and puffy, like he'd been crying.

No one will tell me how bad things were, but based on how I feel and how he looks, it must have been bad.

Gotta end this soon. It's taken me four tries to get this far. I'm so tired. They're pumping me full of drugs.

Charlie is ok. I asked after him when I woke up. He also had to have surgery, but the bullet missed his arteries and joints - looks like a clear shot through muscle with no nerve damage.

I don't know what to tell Jim. Don't know what I may have already told him due to the drugs.

This is not good.

Wednesday, April 29, 2015

I'm back in Boston. In the hospital, still. They decided I was doing well enough to transfer me today, but I still require care and intervention. I may need more surgery, they say. At the very least, I lost a lot of blood. I'll probably have to have rehab. Typing is a bitch, but I guess it must not be too bad because I can still do it. But I don't know how much I'll be doing after the pain meds wear off.

Charlie is ok. They released him from the hospital on Sunday. He came to check on me while Jim was there. It was very awkward.

Jim knows, of course, that Charlie saved my life. He admitted to being there when I got shot. He said we were having dinner at the place where I'd been staying for the week. I think he said something like he had been doing work there. He didn't provide too many details, and Jim hasn't brought it up because I've been in the hospital, so I have no idea what he thinks.

Charlie said that we were attacked, without warning. He said he noticed the laser on me, realized what it was, and shoved me aside at the last minute. Our wounds are consistent with him lunging and shoving me out of the way of the shot - his right shoulder and my left.

He said he looked for the shooter after the shot was fired, but didn't see any sign of him. But that I'd reported seeing a suspicious character around this week, and that it might have been the same person.

Charlie's responsible for the fact that I didn't bleed out. He saw the massive amount of blood pooling from my wound, and grabbed a few hemostats when he went for the bandages. He clamped the artery and applied pressure to the wound - if he hadn't, I'd probably be dead now.

I don't know how to thank him. He took a bullet for me. He got me medical care, and applied advanced first aid to keep me alive until the paramedics could arrive. And I'll never forget the way he sprinted from window to window, checking for the shooter to see if he was still out there.

Thinking back on it, I realize that Charlie must have been armed. When he dived toward the table, he was going for a gun under his coat. I feel a little foolish that I didn't have a gun myself. I'm not a full time resident of Vermont yet, and I don't have a gun permit for the state, so it didn't even occur to me to arm myself.

I guess I'm a pretty crappy prepper. Although if I didn't have good first aid supplies, I'd be dead. So I suppose there's something to say for myself.

Now I'm in Boston. Charlie is in Vermont. I've barely spoken to him - just that one visit on Sunday with Jim in the room and me half out-of-it on pain meds. I have no idea what's happening with my house. I don't have my cell phone.

Jim has been pretty great. He's been completely on top of my medical care, and has been visiting me often in the hospital. I was in ICU at first, but tomorrow I think they'll put me in a regular ward (or maybe even release me) so hopefully friends can visit. I kind of hate being here alone with my thoughts. It hurts to type, and I don't know how lucid I am, so I can't work on my ebooks.

I'm in limbo.

May 2015

Friday, May 1, 2015

It's so good to be home. Jim is hovering over me like a nursemaid, but he had to leave to go pick up Ben and take him and Levi to some thing, so I'm on my own for a little while.

The first thing I did was call Charlie. I hardly know what to say, but it was so good to hear his voice after not speaking to him for almost a week. It's kind of crazy how much time we spent talking last week, and how much I miss it now that I'm away.

I thanked him, profusely. He kept brushing it off. Eventually, he got quiet, and when he did speak, his voice was low and broken-sounding. He said: "I'd never forgive myself if something happened to you." We both went silent, because I didn't know what to say back.

Well, there was nothing I could say, anyway, because I'm married and my husband has been taking meticulous care of me since he got the call that I was shot.

Anyway. Charlie says that once the crime scene had been cleared, he arranged to have the window glass replaced and got the place cleaned up. I think I'll need to replace the couch, because I lost so much blood and there's no way it'll all come out. He splattered blood all over the house, too, when he was checking the windows, but he said it cleaned up ok.

Of course, he didn't have to do any of it - yet another thing for me to thank him for, when I don't know the first thing to say in thanks.

He said that once his shoulder heals up, he'll get back to the projects on my house. In the meantime, he's having David the electrician come in and do as much of the work as possible. The generators came in this week, and Charlie really should have installed them himself so Dave could do the wiring, but he wrangled David into helping, and the two of them got things in place. And I think David is helping him install the appliances, too, even though he didn't have to. I guess he's looking out for his buddy, but I appreciate it regardless.

So I think the main stuff that still needs doing is the rest of the windows, the insulation and the solar collector. And the wood stove. And... I don't even know. More stuff.

But the solar system is in place! It's not running at full capacity, but since no-one is living there right now anyway, it's generating more electricity than the house is using, so the power company is buying it back. I might just sever the connection to the power company now that the solar is up and running, but I feel like I should get some use data and see how much capacity it really provides over time. No idea if a rainy stretch or the snowy winter will interfere with production enough to cut me off. I should know what I need and make any other modifications I have to make before cutting off the grid entirely.

What about whoever shot us? No idea. So far, the police haven't shared any leads with me. Charlie said he didn't see any cars go up or down the driveway, and I think we would have noticed the motion sensor lights coming on, so I guess whoever did it must have walked up and parked somewhere else. So maybe it was the creep with the flashlight, and maybe he was casing the place all along.

I hate that I'm not there, and he could be doing who-knows-what up there. Charlie wouldn't admit to staying at the house, but I can check the ADT alarm code arms and disarms, so I know he's staying there at night. I want to ask him if he at least has a friend staying with him - someone who can help if the guy comes back (or provide first aid if Charlie is the one who's more seriously injured) but I don't know how to ask without telling him I'm watching the security system check-ins. He doesn't want to tell me, and I don't want to put him on the spot about knowing.

So now there's yet another person I care about who I'm keeping secrets from.

The police said they'll do extra patrols in the area, and send someone out to check on it from time to time, but they're stretched thin over a lot of ground, so I doubt they'd be out very often.

I kind of want to go check the creepy contractor out - see if he drives a red truck with a "Vermont Strong" front license plate, and if he owns a gun with a laser sight, but I'm in no position to drive anywhere right now.

We did give all the info to the police, who presumably will do their job and check out the leads. But even if the guy does drive that truck and does own a gun with a laser sight, I suppose it's all circumstantial at this point. We didn't see him there on the property. I don't know of any evidence that puts him there.

For all I know, whoever did this is going to walk away without ever being caught.

I can't decide if it bothers me more that he won't be caught (and punished), or that he's still running around out there. I can't imagine bringing Ben up there if there's some crazy guy running around with a gun. I would never let harm like that come to my son.

I definitely need to get a Vermont gun license. And maybe take up sport shooting. I'm no slouch - I've had to shoot rats with a BB pistol here in the city, when we lived in a crappy apartment years ago - but that's no substitute for potentially taking on an armed human who means me harm.

Wednesday, May 6, 2015

Ben is being so sweet with me since I got home. I was away for a week in Vermont, and then I was in the hospital for almost a week, so it's the longest I've been away from him - ever, really. Jim is trying to downplay the risk to life and limb, but obviously it was serious or I wouldn't have been in the hospital for so long - or be so limited in what I can do now - and Ben can see that. He's always offering to get me snacks - cheese and crackers is his favorite, because he gets to snag some, too. Followed by potato chips. He keeps trying to share his pudding cups with me, and saying I need chicken soup, because those are his favorite foods when he's sick, and that's the only way he can relate to my injury. It's funny and sweet, and I love him so much.

Jim is acting the part of the perfect husband. He works from home when he doesn't have any meetings or office tasks that need his attention, so he can look after me and deal with Ben's coming-home-from-school rituals. Levi's parents have also been great at letting the kids come to their place - I'm going to owe them a major thank-you basket. Lita has been going to doggie day care a lot, because she's just too much for me to handle while I'm injured. Fortunately, the place where I've been taking her for training offers sort of a "train and play" package - they work with her on the basics while she's there - so we've been taking her there, even though it's farther away than our local doggie daycare spot. She still needs work, and I feel better that her training isn't being completely neglected, even if I'm not the one doing it.

One unexpected side effect of all this is that Jim is starting to see just how much I do at home. Between looking after Ben (and Levi, when he's here), getting food on the table, doing dishes and laundry and cleaning the house… it's a lot harder to get work done. He's been working late into the night to try to catch up, or working during the day and staying up late to clean and do house chores, and he's been going out of his way to tell me how he didn't realize how much I've been doing and how much he's coming to appreciate my contributions to the household.

He's also been amazing with helping me change the bandages, staying clean and dressing. I can't really do showers right now, so I'm taking baths, but I need help with my hair since I effectively only have one hand and have to keep my left shoulder dry. Honestly, I'm thinking about getting a really short haircut to make things easier. It'd be more practical, anyway, when SHTF and water and power become more precious.

I've only checked in once with Charlie since I talked with him last Friday. It's been really hard not to call him more often, but I'm not home alone very much and I don't want to deal with calling him in front of Jim. I miss him more than I could have imagined. Our one chat was pretty brief and perfunctory - he gave me a quick rundown on the outstanding projects - but there was a lot more I wanted to say, and it felt like he wanted to say more, too. I've gotta decide what to do about this soon, because the way things are right now is no good for either of us.

Life is very confusing right now.

Friday, May 8, 2015

Ugh.

I'm starting to do more - I left the house this week when Becca came to take me to get my hair cut (on the bright side, the short haircut is really cute)… but apparently that means Jim feels I'm well enough to be chauffeured to marriage counseling. After all, both of these things are "just sitting in a chair for an hour."

I have very mixed feelings about today's counseling session.

Jim was… surprising. He spoke very movingly about how much he's been taking my contributions to our life for granted - and how he couldn't see that until he tried to do some of the stuff I've been doing on top of his regular workload. At least now he really seems to genuinely forgive me for the small stuff I missed that started our marriage issues to begin with. I'm happy about that.

He also spoke about how upset he was when he got the phone call that I'd been shot, and was in surgery, and he needed to come to the hospital as soon as possible. Apparently, while he knew things were getting bad, he hadn't really internalized how much our marriage was suffering until that moment, when it shook him out of his apathy and made him see that he really wants to work at getting things back on track. It was touching, truly.

But I'm tired of hiding things. We can't really fix our marriage unless we're both making an honest effort. I thought that keeping secrets from him was the best way to handle it - that I could show him what I've been working toward once it's all ready and he'd understand my vision in a way he couldn't when it was just a bunch of abstract ideas that he called 'paranoia.'

After spending time with Charlie, it's clear to me that's not happening. Charlie didn't dismiss my concerns out of hand. In fact, he saw the value in being prepared for emergencies, even if not to the extreme degree I want to be prepared.

I realized - I was trying to manipulate Jim. I wanted to present my case in the best possible light in a way that would convince him, when I wasn't able to convince him solely based on the merit of my ideas. But now I've put us in an impossible position - I've bought an entire house and property in the next state, so there's really no backing down from this one if he doesn't agree. And why should I have to back down anyway, if I believe that what I'm doing is the best thing for my family?

It's an impossible situation.

So I... started to get into it. I admitted that I've been keeping things from Jim. I swore that at the time, I thought that what I was doing was right - that he'd agree with me once he could see what I've been working on. But in light of recent happenings, I've now come to see that's not the best way to handle things.

Jim has been amazing, and I've been feeling guiltier and guiltier for keeping such big secrets from him.

He looked stricken when I admitted that. He asked if it had anything to do with the fact that I was having dinner with a strange man when I was shot. I said that it did, but probably not in the way that he thought - because I'm assuming, based on his face and the way he asked, so carefully - that he fears I've been having an affair.

Anyway, I said that I'd rather show him than tell him. That it would make more sense if he could see things for himself. So we agreed that tomorrow, we'd drive up to Vermont. I want to bring Ben, too, because I think he'll love it, but Jim is too worried about what's going on. So Ben will be spending the weekend with Levi.

After that, I didn't dare call Charlie to warn him. I'd like to have some idea of the state that the house is in, or at least warn him to stay away - but I couldn't risk calling him after admitting to Jim that I've been keeping secrets. He'd think the worse.

Speaking of that, I've only spoken to Charlie once this week, but again, it was very perfunctory. Sounds like he's making progress on the house again. We were both careful about what we said, but I admitted that I've missed talking with him. I didn't plan on saying anything to him - it just slipped out. I was trying to keep things distant and professional between us until I figure out what's going on with my marriage - I owe it to all of us to be sure before I do anything else. But apparently intentions don't count for a whole lot when I'm on an 'honesty' kick.

He said he's missed it, too. And there was a long pause, during which neither of us dared to say anything more revealing. Just as well, because I fear how I would have responded. This has gotten so complicated.

I'm excited and a little scared to show Jim the house tomorrow. I don't know how he'll react. We've got an emergency counseling session scheduled for Monday... hopefully things aren't too bad.

Sunday, May 10, 2015

It's Mother's Day. It's been thirteen years since I lost my mother. Jim sent his mom a big bouquet for the day.

I got one, too. I think Jim must have arranged it before we went up to Vermont. It had a card that thanked me for being such an amazing mom. Somehow, I doubt he feels that way right now.

I can't do this today. Need more time.

Tuesday, May 12, 2015

Jim's back at work today. I'm on my own to fend for myself. I'm still not supposed to be driving, so some of the other parents are taking care of transporting Ben. And Jim's still doing a lot of the chores. But for the first time since being shot, I've had an entire day to myself.

Can't say I like it.

This weekend didn't go as well as I'd hoped, but I guess I could say it went as well as I expected.

When we got to the property, Jim stopped the car in the driveway and just sat there. Eventually, he said something sarcastic, like "Is this where I can expect to be greeted by your lover?" There was so much pain in his voice, though, that I couldn't hold it against him, even if it was an arsey thing to say.

Well, as best as I can remember, this is the conversation that followed:

Me: "No. This is the project I've been working so hard on. This house is ours. It sits on fifteen acres of land that is also ours. I've been working with a contractor to add a solar system, make the house more energy efficient, and set up water and sewage systems so we can live completely off the grid if we needed to."

Long pause. Finally, Jim responds: "How? How could you possibly make all this happen without me knowing? For starters, where did all the money come from?"

Me: "I'm so proud of that. Most of it came from the ebooks I've been writing. I actually quit all of my clients months ago, because my ebooks have been bringing in so much cash. I did borrow a little from our retirement account when I bought the house, so I'd have enough cash left over to do the work on the property, but it wasn't too much and we should be able to pay it off when we sell our Boston house. Or, in time, I can pay it back from my writing income."

Jim: "You took money from our retirement account? Without even discussing it with me?"

Me: "Not that much - only around $50,000. We can easily repay that if we sell our house in Boston, or I can repay it on my own before too much longer - by the end of the year, for sure, or maybe sooner if the rest of the work on the house doesn't eat up too much of my income."

Jim: "You bought a house. Without talking to me about it. You took money from our retirement account. Without talking to me about it. What where you possibly thinking, Della?" (By this point, he was practically yelling. I did not like it.)

Me: "I was thinking that this is a perfect place for our family if something bad happens. It's already set up to grow food. It's back away from the road on a sizable chunk of property, so it's hidden and there's plenty of room for us. It's defensible. And because it has a river and a small pond, and plenty of room for solar panels, it's easy to make it sustainable for off-grid living. I was thinking this was the best thing I could do to protect you and Ben, and make it possible for us to survive something horrible - and even thrive - when other people just aren't prepared."

Jim: "That again. I thought you had given up that nonsense."

Me: "No. I don't think it's nonsense. There's plenty of information I could show you about various disasters. We had a close brush with Ebola. Russia is doing crazy things. ISIS is planning more and more elaborate and horrifying attacks. There are so many things-"

Jim: "Enough. I've seen and heard enough. This is ridiculous. It was ridiculous when you wanted to stockpile on groceries at home, and it's grown beyond comprehension with you buying a whole fucking house out in the middle of nowhere, so far from home it's practically in Canada!"

I took a deep breath and counted to ten while I tried to keep from exploding back at him. "Let me just show you around. It's such a great place, I really think you and Ben would like it here."

He shook his head. "We're done here."

But then, he slammed his hand on the steering wheel. "This is where you were? You were here, working on this place, when you told me you were at a 'writer's retreat?'"

I nodded. "Yeah, but it wasn't entirely a lie. This place is great for writing."

His voice got dangerously quiet then. "And that guy. Charlie. What was he doing here?"

Me: "Charlie is the contractor who's working on the house. He's actually been really great about making useful suggestions and steering me in the right direction for more information, and he let me watch him doing some of the work and answered my million questions, so I should be able to fix pretty much anything he's installed. I made him dinner to thank him for all the work, and for being so patient with my questions."

I didn't tell him *everything.* For some reason, I was still holding out hope that he'd come to like the place, so I wasn't ready to admit the creepy guy had been lurking around. Or that Charlie had been spending the night. I did't want to muddy the waters even more. We clearly had enough issues to work through without that.

Jim: "Are you *fucking* that guy?"

Well, of course I was horrified then. And angry. Because whatever might have happened if the shooter hadn't chosen the moment we kissed to attack me, *that* didn't happen.

Me: "No. But the fact that you'd ask me that - and in that tone with those words - tells me how much our marriage is suffering."

Jim: "Suffering? Hah. You've just dragged our marriage out into the country and SHOT it."

And that was it. Without another word, he turned on the car, switched into reverse so fast that he spun the wheels in the mud and for a horrible moment it looked like we'd get stuck - and then hightailed it out of there.

The drive home was three hours. He didn't say a word the entire time. When we got back, he dropped me off at home and left again, without even getting out of the car. I assume he went to spend the night at Ari's.

I didn't see him again until Sunday night, when he brought Ben home from Levi's and acted like everything was ok. He was done being nice, though. He barely spoke two words to me. He did offer to help me check my dressings, because I can't do it by myself with only one hand, but he was not gentle or tender or nice about it - it was perfunctory.

I resisted the urge to call Charlie. I wanted nothing more than to talk to him - admit that I'd fessed up about the property to Jim and how badly he'd taken it. I wanted Charlie to tell me it was all right, and that Jim was being unreasonable - but it wouldn't have been right to put Charlie in that place. Or to seek validation from him. Whatever there is between me and Charlie is between me and Charlie. Dragging Jim into it isn't fair to Charlie, and I don't want Jim tangled up in any way in my feelings for Charlie.

Well, we've had two marriage counseling sessions since I told Jim about the house - one Monday, and one today.

I think our marriage is over.

He won't even contemplate my side of things. The counselor said that now everything is out in the open, we really need to focus on seeing the other person's side of things and thinking about how we move forward as a couple.

I can see, from his side of things, it would seem strange that I made the decisions I did without talking with him. I guess it does seem a little crazy that I'd buy a house without even suggesting the idea to him.

But from my side, I know why I did it. I did it so we'd have a place where we could all be safe together.

The marriage counselor kept emphasizing that. That I didn't buy the house to get away from my family - that I did it because I believed I was doing something to keep us safe. That I did it because I love my family and was trying to take care of us.

Jim just talked about how that proves I'm crazy, and he can't be married to a crazy person. And his son can't be living with a crazy person.

That kind of talk gives me chills. I've been beginning to realize that my marriage may have serious problems. Maybe it is broken beyond repair. A few months ago, I would have been heartbroken to even contemplate such an idea… but today, I don't see it as the worse thing in the world. It happens to people all the time. If it happened to us, I suppose we'd deal with it and move forward however our new reality works. I don't doubt it would be hard, and probably painful - but I don't think it would kill me.

But never once, since I've begun to contemplate the fact that our marriage really may be broken, has it occurred to me that he might try to take my son away from me.

No. Freaking. Way.

Ben is the light of my life. My whole life has been about caring for that boy since he was born. I was thrilled to be able to work from home when I started freelancing - I could be a mom and a professional - but it was always mom first. If there wasn't enough time in the day, it was my work that took a back seat - not my son. Everything I do is about making sure he has the best possible life. Even buying this property - it's been about keeping him safe if something horrible happens. Having a place for us to live, when other people who aren't prepared go the way of the Dodo bird.

Since I got shot, Jim has spent so much time talking about all the work I do to keep the house running. He's seen how difficult it is to take care of Ben, get him where he needs to go when he needs to be there, and make sure he has the love and attention he needs. And doing that around a full-time job? Is nigh impossible. That's why I was burning the candle at both ends for so many months. I was trying to do it all, but I have the luxury of late nights, squeezing in work while Ben is napping or working on homework or at school.

No way could Jim do it and keep his full-time office job.

And no way would I let someone keep my son away from me.

The marriage counselor keeps telling us we shouldn't make a rash decision. That we need to take time to let the anger simmer down, and have a real, logical discussion about how we want to move forward. But Jim doesn't seem to want to let that happen.

I don't know what to do.

Monday, May 18, 2015

What. The. Fuck.

What the actual FUCK.

I got served.

Jim is filing for custody of Ben. Sole custody. He alleges that I have mental health issues that prevent me from being a suitable parent.

What the fuck!

But it gets better. I also got served an Order to Vacate Marital Home.

Some asshole judge granted Jim a temporary Order to Vacate Marital Home. I consulted a lawyer, and the only way the judge will force someone out of the marital home is if the requesting party can demonstrate that… "the health, safety or welfare" of the moving party or a minor child in the home is threatened by the presence of the other party.

In other words, he somehow convinced a judge that I represent a threat to my family - so much so that the judge threw out the initial notice period and issued an immediate temporary order. I have a few days to respond, but as of now, I have to be out of the house. And apparently this is a serious order - kind of like a restraining order - and I can face big trouble if I violate it. It would pretty much guarantee that I'd lose the custody case if I made a big to-do over this.

So for the moment, I've taken my laptop and a bag full of clothes and left the house. I'm staying in a hotel. I called Ari and asked if I could stay there, but he said he doesn't want to get in the middle of this and me staying there would be forcing him to pick a side. I kind of feel like him telling me I can't stay there IS picking a side - Jim's side. But I've got bigger things to worry about right now.

Like finding a lawyer and dealing with this custody thing.

Tuesday, May 19, 2015

I am absolutely heartbroken. I called Jim to ask if I could at least talk to Ben. I wanted to ask how his day was, and tell him I love him, and wish him a good night. Jim didn't even take my call. I left a message, and a few minutes later, he texted me back saying that he "didn't think that would be a good idea" as I was "too unstable and unpredictable."

What the FUCK!

Of course, I started to send an angry text back… but then I realized that anything I send to him in writing (even the voicemail I left him) could be used against me in the custody hearing.

So I restrained myself.

But it was SO HARD!

I did start a new file on my computer, and I typed all the mean, angry things I wanted to say to him about all this bullshit. Hopefully I've hidden it well enough that it doesn't come up if someone subpoenas my laptop.

Maybe I should get a backup laptop for stuff I don't want the court to see.

Now that I think about it, it might not be a bad idea for me to transfer this diary over. I don't think it paints me in too bad of a light, but there are things I don't want to fight with Jim about.

Like Charlie.

I still need to call Charlie. I haven't told him about any of this. I'm too angry right now, and I know if I find a sympathetic ear I'll unload on the unlucky recipient. I don't want that to be him.

I sent him a text last week saying that things had gotten very complicated, and that I might be out of touch for a week or two. But that I look forward to speaking with him again when the timing is better. He said that he understood, and there's no rush and no pressure - he'll be happy to speak with me when I'm ready. I know that talking to him would make this so much easier… but I don't want to fall right into something right now. It doesn't feel right.

Wednesday, May 20, 2015

Well, I've got a lawyer. We've filed an objection on the Order to Vacate, and on the motion for sole custody. The lawyer says he doesn't understand how Jim could have convinced a judge to actually issue an Order to Vacate based on the disagreement we've had - and that being prepared for emergency situations doesn't constitute mental illness. So hopefully we'll be able to resolve all this relatively soon. But I don't know what I'll say once I move back into the house. I really don't want to be anywhere near Jim right now, but I miss my boy so much. Somehow it feels worse than when I went to Vermont for the week - then, I was choosing to be away, but I could have left at any point and been back with my baby within a few hours. Now I'm being forced to stay away, and I want nothing more than to give my little guy a hug and cook him dinner and listen to him talk about his day at school. I actually miss helping him with his homework.

And the dog! Jim's got the nerve to keep the damn dog. I bought the dog, I've been the one training her and everything - but he says Ben is completely attached to her and that taking her away on top of me being gone would be just too much for him. I told the lawyer that Jim was pissed when I got the dog, and has basically wanted nothing to do with her, but he says that the less I do against Ben's interests, the better for the custody hearing. So I have to let him keep the dog because it shows I'm putting Ben's happiness first.

I've got a hearing tomorrow on the temporary order to vacate the house. So hopefully I'll be back home by tomorrow night.

Thursday, May 21, 2015

Shit. Shit, shit, fuck.

That did NOT go as planned.

Had the hearing today regarding the order to vacate. Not only did the judge refuse to reverse the order - he changed it from temporary to 90 days, with the option for Jim to extend it basically indefinitely.

In other words, I'm not going home.

I've got a temporary custody hearing the week after next, but until then, Jim effectively has sole custody of Ben. I can't go to the house. The school has been instructed not to release him to me. (So embarrassing! How will I ever explain this to them after we get it all resolved?)

This is FUCKED UP.

I guess there's no point in me staying in Boston right now. I may as well be saving the money I'm spending on hotels and head up to the place in Vermont. It feels like I'm turning tail and running away, but the lawyer assures me I don't want to make waves right now. I don't want to risk screwing this up.

I'll spend the night here and head up to Vermont in the morning. I guess I don't need to bother Charlie - I'll get there in plenty of time to find him still working at the house tomorrow. Not that I have the slightest clue what to do when I see him.

It'll be the first time I've seen him - really seen him - since that night. Since he saved my life. Was it really almost a month ago?

His quick visit in the hospital doesn't count. Jim was there, and I was on painkillers - I couldn't say what I wanted to say.

But what would I have wanted to say if I could?

Well, shit. Now I'm going to be thinking not only about how screwed I am on the custody hearing, but what to say to Charlie tomorrow when I see him again.

Friday, May 22, 2015

So it turns out Charlie's not working on my house anymore. Apparently he got done sometime this week, but because I wasn't in touch with him, he didn't want to bother me. So he wasn't here when I arrived… so I was alone in the house.

I didn't realize how terrifying I'd find it after what happened.

I called him, and told him I'm here at the house. He said he's at a job site, but he'll come by when he's done for the day.

I don't really want to be alone there, so I headed out to a local restaurant for lunch. They recognized me as the woman who got shot. It's a small town, and stuff like that doesn't happen around here very often. Also, Charlie is a local favorite, so the fact that he saved some city woman's life has been making the rounds.

I've been hanging out here for most of the afternoon. In a little bit, I'll go get some groceries. Even if I don't end up cooking dinner for Charlie, I need groceries to have at the house. But if he's going be there after a job… well, if he stays for more than a few minutes, he's going to need food. Maybe I should just cook something anyway, just in case. If he doesn't stay, I can always eat the leftovers for lunch tomorrow.

Saturday, May 23, 2015

Charlie came by after he was done working last night, as promised.

We spent a long time talking.

I told him about what's been going on with Jim - the divorce and custody stuff. I told him I wasn't trying to get sympathy, and I didn't really need a reaction from him at all, but I just wanted him to know what's been going on and why I'm here.

Also… I admitted to him that our chats the last time I was here meant a lot to me. And that I had been deeply attracted to him. I'm sure he knew that, after the kiss, but I wanted to put it out there.

But I said that nothing can come of that right now, because I'm embroiled in a very messy divorce - and the future of my relationship with my child is on the line. So regardless of how either of us may feel, I need things to stay platonic between us.

I guess that was presuming a lot. It sorta strikes me that way now, looking at the words I've typed out. But after what he said that time on the phone… and the kiss… and the fact that he saved my life… I guess it's reasonably safe to assume he'd be interested in more, if I was in a position to pursue it.

Anyway.

I also admitted to him that I was a little terrified of being here by myself after what happened. He said that he completely understood that, and asked what he could do. I want to look into a more serious perimeter security system - I did a quick search and found something about a buried wire system that tells you if someone violates the perimeter. But even if I know someone is poking around the property, there's not much I can do about it.

Given the pending divorce and custody hearing, and the allegations of mental health issues, now would be a very bad time to apply for a gun permit and buy a gun. So I really can't afford to pursue any method of defending myself. I guess I could try to rig up some traps, and maybe a panic room I can flee to if something strikes me as off - but I can't take any active steps to protect myself.

Well, now that I think about it, if I want this house to be ready for a serious emergency, I should have a panic room anyway. So I've gotta work on that.

In the meantime, I asked if Charlie would be willing to stay here at night - on the DL. I don't know if Jim would hire surveillance to try to get more dirt on me, but given how far he's taking things, I wouldn't put it past him. So having Charlie's truck around, or having it be general knowledge that he's staying here, could potentially be a problem. We'll have to figure out a better long-term system, but for now, he's going to drive his truck home and then have a friend drop him off.

I feel so much better knowing he's going to be here. I know nothing can happen between us right now, and it may be difficult to refrain from those amazing late night conversations - or anything else - but my son is my first priority. I can't do anything to jeopardize that. But it's really comforting to know Charlie will be around.

I need to figure out a long-term solution to this issue if there's any chance of bringing Ben here. I don't want to live in Boston, I know that. But if Jim and I are really getting a divorce, I need this to be a safe place for my son. Which means that whoever shot me has got to be removed.

Wednesday, May 27, 2015

Making progress. I've selected a perimeter security system. I've gone with the low-profile buried wire system. I think the fence systems are a bit too flashy - they're more inclined to make people think there's something here that needs protecting. The buried wire is invisible, but still gives me plenty of warning if people come back here. Plus the wire is a lot cheaper and faster - fencing in 15 acres would cost a fortune and take a while to finish.

I'm also putting a gate across the driveway. I'm going with a low-profile livestock-style gate, and a no trespassing sign. It won't actually do anything to stop the determined invader, but it will deter the casual Looky Loo, and it'll buy me the few extra seconds of warning that it would take someone to get out of the car, open the gate and drive through.

And of course, I've got a hidden security camera in the trees with a clear view of the gate and anyone who might be trying to open it. And an audible chime in the house when someone opens the gate, kind of like a doorbell.

No point in going small.

For a panic room, I think I found a company that can build one in the basement. Basically, they'll wall off one side of the basement, and create a secure room there. Then we'll put a fake facade over the front of it that will look like the rest of the basement wall, and we'll figure out some way to hide the door. That way, if someone does get into the house and pokes around in the basement, nothing will stand out.

I'm pondering putting racks of shelves down there to hold my preps. Then, to get to the back wall where the panic room door is located, you'd have to go through a maze of racks. That'll make it easier to hide the door, too - maybe I can put a swing-out rack in front of it, or something. I'll figure it out.

Unfortunately, it's going to take time to get this stuff done. I really don't feel comfortable here in the meantime. I've never seen anyone poking around here during the day, but that doesn't mean the person who shot me couldn't buck the trend and come after me in broad daylight. It would certainly be unexpected in light of the prior nighttime encounters.

Charlie picked up a small dirt bike, so he could get out here through the woods without anyone seeing him and without his truck being here in

the drive. It means a lot to me that he'd go through so much trouble, and
that he's willing to stay here to make me feel better.

We've been carefully avoiding any physical contact, or any discussions
that might veer into the realm of the emotional. We've also been pretty
good about not spending the night chatting away every night - it's hard to
function on no sleep day after day, and I feel like that could lead to the
other stuff we've been avoiding. But it's impossible to stop it altogether.
One of us will bring up something completely innocuous, and hours
later, we'll find that we've been jabbering away. It's sort of wonderful and
hopeless at the same time.

Realistically, though, I'm not sure what to do long-term about my
security here. This is a small town, and people have known that I'm back
since I hung out in the restaurant last Friday. News travels fast.

So if my attacker is a local - and I'll assume that he is because who else
would even stumble across this property? - he knows I'm back.

I'm trying to keep it from being general knowledge that Charlie is
staying at my place, but who knows how well we've succeeded at that?
He's put some lights on timers at his place, so it looks like he's there at
night, but I'm not sure if anyone's getting fooled.

I hadn't counted on this aspect of small-town living. When I chose this
property, it seemed to check all the marks for sustainability and long-term
survival in a disaster situation. What I did not think about is the fact that
pretty much everyone in town knows it's here - and knows I'm here - and
what's to stop them from helping themselves to my bounty if things go
bad?

More urgently, though - how do I protect myself from someone who
presumably knows I'm here?

Logically, it makes sense to be somewhere else. But I want to be here
while the security stuff is being installed, and I need to be close enough to
Boston to get back down there for the custody hearings.

I could try staying at Charlie's place, instead, but his house is in town
and everyone would know I'm there pretty quick. Although maybe the
attacker would be less likely to come after me in town, with all those
people around. On the other hand, though, it could be bad for my case if
it looks like I'm suddenly living with some strange guy that my son has
never even met.

Friday, May 29, 2015

Perimeter security installed. I know it doesn't actually protect me - just alerts me when someone crosses onto my property - but I feel a lot more secure with that in place. The thought of someone creeping around on my property in the dark is incredibly unnerving. And being shot, out of nowhere, while I thought I was safe in the comfort of my own home… that's been pretty traumatic, to say the least.

This helps.

I also really appreciated the discretion of the security firm. They have an option for their personnel to wear utility uniforms, and to wrap their van to look like a utility van, so it just looks like I was having some simple utility work done if anyone was watching the property. It may be paranoia, but there's definitely someone out to get me, so I feel it's pretty justified.

The panic room construction has begun. We've changed things up a little bit from my original plans, but I'm not going to write too much about it in case someone ever gets ahold of my laptop and discovers my diary. Again, paranoia, but it would be pretty damn useless for me to spend all this money and effort on a safe room, only to reveal its location and how to access it if someone hell-bent on doing harm to my family happens to get ahold of my laptop.

Or break into my cloud storage account, actually. Damnit. Maybe I need to look into more secure options for that, too…

Well, anyway. It's going to take a few weeks based on the options I've chosen. Our custody hearing is next week, so I think I'll spend the week in Boston - it'll get me away from here and I'll feel better for being gone. I don't know why I haven't seen any signs of activity from the gunman, and maybe I am sick in the head for wishing for something… but it just feels ominous that he's been so absent. Like he's planning something bigger.

Or maybe all the activity has scared him away.

Or maybe he's afraid of getting caught so he's backing off for now.

Who the Hell knows? I don't know why he was out here in the first place, and I have no idea why he'd shoot me, so trying to speculate about why he's staying away now is an exercise in futility.

June 2015

Tuesday, June 2, 2015

YAY! I am SO RELIEVED! There aren't enough exclamation points and capitals in the world to express how happy I am right now.

We had the custody hearing today. The judge was actually quite reasonable. He said that the picture that Jim had painted of me was of some raving lunatic, but that when I presented my side of the argument, he actually found me quite logical and well-reasoned.

Granted, he said that I had been making some really questionable decisions, but he pointed out that he's not ruling on the divorce - only on custody - and that it was very apparent that I love my son and am no danger to him. Thank GOD. (Or whomever is out there… my sincere gratitude for today.)

The judge further said that Jim's allegations of neglect are pretty much negligible. (Hah!) Forgetting to pick him up once, and missing a few of his activities, apparently doesn't constitute neglect unless Ben was repeatedly left in unsafe situations, or unless I was failing to do the really important stuff, like feeding him and getting him off to school everyday. Since that wasn't the case, the neglect charges are groundless. Although the judge did say he'd want to revisit this in a few months to make sure conditions hadn't changed, and invited either of us to request an emergency hearing if we felt that Ben's safety was in question. But he gave Jim a stern warning about wasting the court's time just because he wasn't getting along with me.

However, because of the Order to Vacate, I'm still not allowed to live at home with Ben and Jim. And the judge thinks it's in his best interest to stay in Boston - at least when school is in session - because it's less disruptive to his life. Even though I've been the primary caregiver historically. I'm not so thrilled about that.

So the deal we've made is for shared legal and physical custody. Ben will be free to spend most of the summer with me in Vermont (if he likes it), but he'll be living in Boston during the school year. I'm free to get him on weekends, and have two weeknight visits per week… but that's going to be complicated unless the divorce judge lifts the Order to Vacate.

My attorney said we can file a motion to get the Order to Vacate lifted, based on the custody judge's assessment that I am not a threat to Ben. He says we should order an independent evaluation of me by a third-party psychiatrist just to prove that I'm not mentally unfit, but I know I'll pass that with flying colors, so I'm hopeful we can get the ruling overturned.

Not that I particularly want to return to living in my marital home, but I want to be with Ben - I've been missing him so much - and part of me wants to stick it to Jim for trying to fuck with me.

For now, Ben has basically the rest of June to go in the school season. The last day of school is June 25. Then, he's spending four weeks at camp - starting the day after school gets out. In the past, we've done two weeks and three weeks, but he loves it so much that he begged for four weeks this year. We already made the arrangements before all of this happened. Now I'm not going to be selfish and take away his fun just because I want to spend time with him.

So that means he won't be done at camp until July 25. If we can get the Order to Vacate lifted in the next few weeks, I suppose I can spend some time with him at home before he goes. But in the meantime, I'm not bringing him back to Vermont for the weekends until I figure out some way to keep him safe. I'll just let him stay home for the rest of the school year, and we'll start his time in Vermont when he gets out of camp.

That gives me not quite eight weeks to figure out who shot me, and make sure he's no longer a threat.

Friday, June 5, 2015

So far, so good. I've done the independent evaluation with the psychiatrist, and he said he sees no reason to consider me mentally unwell. He says that my prepper concerns may be a little unconventional, but that emergency preparedness isn't grounds to find someone mentally unstable. Even if most people would think the emergencies I'm worried about (and my preparations to keep us safe) are a little extreme. As long as I'm not acting erratically or exhibiting signs of true paranoia - which I'm not, thank you very much - it's all good.

He did suggest that I might want to continue counseling, though, based on the stress of going through a divorce, the hostile custody hearing - and the fact that I was shot and nearly killed about six weeks ago. I did admit that I'd been feeling unsafe in my home in Vermont, and had been taking steps to improve the safety situation there, like installing better security measures and putting in a safe room. He said that given what happened, taking those precautions seemed like a reasonable reaction. But that it's not good to feel unsafe in your own home - it can be stressful and can lead to unexpected or erratic behavior. And a bunch of other psychobabble feel good crap.

Honestly, I'm not so sure how I feel about therapy after my marriage counseling failed so spectacularly. Although I suppose I shouldn't blame that on the therapist - first, it was Jim just going through the motions that meant we weren't making strides, and then, he got too angry with me to give it a chance. (Well, ok, if I'm honest, I guess me keeping secrets didn't help. I'm so angry at how he's blown everything up that it's easy to shrug off my share of the blame, but if I'm going to be a good example for my son, I need to own up to my bullshit. Even if it's only in my own diary.)

Anyway, I think the marriage counseling actually did help me. So maybe it's not the worst thing in the world if I did start seeing a therapist to help me get through this rough patch and find some healthy ways of coping with feeling unsafe in my home.

Speaking of feeling safe in my home - it turns out you don't have to have a gun license to own or carry a gun in Vermont. Whoa! Regulations are so strict here in Massachusetts that it didn't even occur to me I might be able to buy a handgun for self-defense without going through a big process. Apparently you can walk right into a shop with your state-issued photo ID and buy a firearm (provided you pass an FBI background check). Maybe that's why Charlie was so casual about carrying.

I think I should hold off until I have a hearing about overturning the Order to Vacate, but maybe next week I can buy a firearm and have something around the house for self-protection. That would make me feel SO MUCH BETTER about staying in my own home.

Combine that with the fact that I'll have the panic room in another week or two, and I might feel safe enough to let poor Charlie go back to his own life. He must find it a big hassle to sneak over to my place every night and back again every morning. Although I guess once these hearings are done, it doesn't have to be such a big secret.

I'll head back up to Vermont for the weekend - see how things are going with the panic room (and save some cash on hotels because Boston is ridiculously expensive on the weekends) but I'll be back next week for the hearing on the Order to Vacate. If it gets overturned, maybe I can swing by the house and pick up some more of my stuff, and visit with Ben for a while, before moving up to the new house full-time.

I guess that means I can apply for a resident ID. Wow. Not how I expected any of this to go down even a few months ago. This is a crazy year.

Sunday, June 7, 2015

Shit, shit, shit.

I was just starting to relax my guard a little, but the creep came back.

I'm still shaking just writing about it, even though it was all over more than twelve hours ago.

Charlie was here and we were just sitting down to a dinner we'd cooked together. We've gotten a little more lax about lights at night now that I've got the perimeter security system up and running. Sure enough, my trusty little system worked like a champ, sending an audible chirp through the house when the perimeter was violated.

I felt my stomach clench, and it felt like I'd been dunked into an ice water bath, but we sprang into action. Charlie killed the lights, and I ran to the room where I've got the video feed set up. Sure enough, there was a pickup truck driving through the gate. I couldn't tell if it was red because it was so dark, and I was watching an IR feed, but when I zoomed in, I saw the same "Vermont Strong" license plate we'd seen before.

The bastard didn't bother to close the gate behind him - I'm guessing he left it open for a quick getaway.

A moment later, I was calling the police and Charlie appeared at my side, watching the feeds with me. I could barely dial - I was shaking - so Charlie took the phone from me and took over. He spoke quietly, explaining the situation, while we watched the truck pull up just beyond the range of the motion sensor light.

I was torn between turning on the flood lights I've installed and lighting the bastard up, or sitting tight to give the cops a chance to get here and maybe arrest the guy. If he's the same guy who shot us - and I just know he is - I'd feel a lot better knowing he's rotting away in jail somewhere versus scaring him off for the moment with a lot of new lighting. Although that might be just as good - maybe I could get a clear shot of him if we turned on the lights, and the cops could track him down at their leisure.

Well, maybe leisure isn't the greatest idea, after all.

Anyway, the decision was taken out of my hands. The guy was out and pacing around the property with his flashlight - but he was being very careful to keep the light from shining into the house - I guess he didn't want to alert us. But I've set up video feeds that cover the entire yard (although looking at them I noticed there was a blind spot behind the barn - gotta deal with that) so we could watch his progress from inside without having to be anywhere near the windows.

Out of the corner of my eye, I saw Charlie pull a handgun from its holster - I don't know where it was earlier in the evening because I hadn't seen any sign of it - and he checked the mag and chambered a round. Then he slipped it back, feeling the safety with his thumb. At that moment, I couldn't decide whether I was more terrified for or attracted to him. I didn't want him to get shot (didn't want either of us to get shot) but it was an incredible turn-on to see that he was ready to protect us. I don't remember ever feeling quite that way about Jim.

Something like a minute passed after Charlie made the call to the police before the guy stopped in the yard for a moment, then the creep turned and hightailed it back to his truck. He pulled out of the drive so fast he peeled out, and I hoped for a second he might get stuck. (Part of me thinks I should pave the drive, but I fear that would attract more attention to this place - leaving it dirt keeps a rustic feel to the property.)

No such luck. He backed right out of the drive and took off down the road. He didn't bother closing the gate (not that I expected him to stop for such a nicety, given the way he took off like a bat out of hell).

We watched for a moment to make sure he was really gone. I think both of us were puzzled by the way he took off. Then, Charlie called the police back to tell them what had happened. Based on the timing, the officer guessed that the guy had a police scanner on him, and took off when he heard the call go out for vehicles to head out to the house.

They still came out to the house, checking the driveway for anything identifiable. They looked at the yard where the guy had been walking, and they reviewed my security tape and asked for a copy for their records. But there wasn't much they could do.

I still don't know how difficult it is for them to look up a red pickup truck registered in the area, and find one that has had a "Vermont Strong" plate issued to it in 2012. Or to look up that contractor guy and see if he's got a red truck registered, because I still think it's been him all along. But they just said they couldn't reveal the details of an ongoing investigation.

Hah.

I bet they haven't touched it since they processed the paperwork after I got shot.

After they left, our dinner had gotten cold and I was still feeling cold and shaky. Charlie said that I was probably still feeling the fight-or-flight reaction. Because I actually got shot last time, it might take a while for me to calm down when I was subjected to a legitimate threat again.

We turned out all the lights, reset the security system, and he held me in the dark while I waited to calm down - or waited for the creep to come back. Eventually, I started to feel warm again. And then… something unexpected happened. I jumped him.

I certainly wasn't planning it. My divorce is really messy, and I'm still fighting with Jim over getting time with Ben. I'm surely not over my marriage, so now is not the time to be getting involved with another guy.

And even if all of those things weren't a factor, I wouldn't have wanted my first time with a guy to be a reaction to such a traumatic event.

But… it was. Right there on the living room floor, in a nest of blankets he'd made to try to keep me warm.

Well, because this is my diary, I guess I can say: it's not how I'd have planned it, but if it were to happen again? I sure wouldn't complain. Maybe my marriage with Jim has been suffering longer than I realized, because I can't remember the last time I felt like *that*.

Rowr.

Tuesday, June 9, 2015

Well, Judge Asshole wasn't quite as much of a douchenozzle as I feared, given the fact that he issued the Order to Vacate in the first place. We had our hearing today, and he reviewed all the evidence - including the independent psychiatric evaluation I had, and the custody judge's conclusion. He asked me a bunch of questions, but in the end, he declared that he could find no reason to continue the Order to Vacate. So he overturned it.

Jim's basically not talking to me, which is pretty much ok as far as I'm concerned right now. I have a feeling that if we were talking, I'd completely unload on him. As much as I know that would feel SO satisfying in the short term, I also know it wouldn't be productive in the long term. He and I have got to figure out how to co-parent our son, and animosity between us is not going to help us improve our communication.

I went back to the house after the order was overturned - with a copy for myself in case he decided to try calling the cops. He followed me back, and then followed me around as I packed up more of my things. My clothes, for example, and some of my books, and a few of my movies. It's almost like he thought I was going to steal something. Hah! As if it's stealing to take stuff from our marital household. It's not like I'm some chick who was shacking up with him for a little while. Our entire lives have been intertwined for nearly a decade and a half. Hell, I'M the one who's been dealing with our finances for the past twelve years - and I'm the one who's responsible for our good credit, and now our flush savings account. Last fall, I remember us being so broke that a car repair wiped us out.

Anyway, Jim is a perfectly competent professional, but he kind of sucks at domestic administration.

Finally, he said: "I've got to get back to work, but I want you gone by the time Ben gets home from school."

"Uh-uh. No dice. We've got joint custody and I've got a right to be in this house. I've been dying to see my son, who you've been keeping from me for weeks. I will be staying here to spend the evening with my son, and I will leave in the morning to go back to my house in Vermont. But I will be back often between now and the end of his school year, and when he gets back from summer camp, he's staying with me in Vermont for as long as he wants - maybe even through the beginning of the next school year."

"We'll see about that," he answered. I thought it sounded pretty ominous. I don't know what other kind of threats he thinks he's going to employ. Maybe *I* should be the one seeking sole custody; maybe *he's* mentally unbalanced.

I suggested that he be there when Ben gets home from school so we can attempt to explain this whole big mess to him - together.

He agreed to that, at least, so he closeted himself in the office to work from home until Ben got back.

That conversation was… tricky. I wanted to be honest with him, but at the same time not burden him with too many details. I wasn't sure how Jim wanted to tackle it. We should have talked about it ahead of time - which just goes to show we need practice at this co-parenting thing.

Everything was so much easier when we were happily married. We always backed each other up in front of the kid. If either of us disagreed with something, we'd discuss it later and come back to Ben with the new ruling. But now, we can barely stand to talk to each other, so there was a lot of awkward backpedaling and looking at one another to try to see whether the other agreed with what we were saying, etc. It was kind of a mess.

In the end, we told him something along the lines of mommy and daddy aren't getting along right now, so we've decided to live in separate houses. I told him that I bought a house up in Vermont, and it was only a few hours away, and we had so much land to run and play - and that Lita would love it. (By the way, I was SO HAPPY to see that damn dog, and she was so happy to see me that she peed a little! Who would have known that after things started out so rocky, we'd actually become such good friends.)

We told him that he'd be living with dad while he was in school, so he could hang out with his friends and do his after school activities and things would still be pretty normal for him. And that I would be around some during the week, too. But that he could spend the weekends in Vermont with me during the next school year - and the entire rest of the summer, after he got back from summer camp.

We both tried to emphasize - a lot - that we loved him, and that this was nothing to do with him. I told him that I like it out in the country, where it's quiet and peaceful and there's room to spread out and the air smells fresh and full of green growing things - but that dad likes it here in the city, where he's close to work and can do anything he feels like doing because the city has all kinds of restaurants and museums and things. I started to tell him a little about how his dad and I are growing apart, and that we value different things, but Jim gave me a really pissy look, so I left it alone.

Now I'm sleeping in the guest room and typing this after Ben has gone to bed, when Jim and I would normally hang out. The house doesn't feel like my home anymore. I've only been gone a few weeks, but now it feels like hostile territory. As much as I don't feel safe in my Vermont house right now, it still feels like more of a home than this place. I can't wait until I get that whole thing figured out and it's safe to bring Ben there. Then it'll really be home.

Also… I miss Charlie. I've been trying so hard not to get attached, and not to develop feelings, because now is not a good time for that. But apparently it's happened in spite of my best intentions. I've sent him a couple of texts, but I'm not going to call him because I don't want Jim or Ben to hear me talking to some guy right now.

It's SO GOOD to be with Ben again. But I don't want to be here. I guess Jim has won that particular battle, after all.

Thursday, June 11, 2015

Last night was… interesting. And informative.

I got back home to Vermont yesterday, so Charlie came over last night. I told him it was time to talk about the things we're not really talking about. He said that was fine by him, as he's just been waiting for me to be ready to have this discussion.

I admitted that I'm falling for him. I told him that the timing wasn't great, but I couldn't deny it when I was hiding in the guest bedroom at my old house, wanting nothing more than to be away from Jim and with Charlie instead. I wanted to wait longer to see if I still feel this way months down the road, when I'm not in the middle of a messy divorce and potentially recovering from the failure of my marriage (and on the rebound). But life is short - I realized that when we both got shot - and I didn't want to let more time go by without at least admitting how I felt.

He was so amazing. He let me get through all of that without interrupting me and without making me feel… I don't know, like a goof, or self-conscious, or whatever. When I'd said my piece, he took me in his arms and ran a hand down the side of my face - it gave me shivers, but the good kind - and told me that I'd just made him so happy, and that he'd been hoping I felt that way, but that he wanted to give me time and didn't want to pry or make me feel awkward about whatever was growing between us. And that admitting our feelings for one another didn't have to mean anything has to happen between us right now. He said he can be patient and wait for me to be ready to take the next step - whatever that next step will be - because he knows that my life is complicated right now and he doesn't want to rush me.

Well, of course I melted into a puddle of goo right there in his arms. I've been with Jim so long that I'd forgotten what it's like to feel those new relationship feelings. And Jim was never really that romantic to begin with. Charlie… he's another beast entirely.

(Did I mention that I'm really enjoying the fact that he's a contractor? Jim and I always had a great intellectual connection, but Charlie and I have had these great conversations… *and* he's got all these delicious muscles and he's so solid from working with his body all day. It feels so Neanderthal to admit how much I like his physique, or the fact that he makes me feel so feminine… but apparently that cave man DNA runs deep because I just can't help myself. And then there was how I felt when he was ready to defend us from that creep roaming around my property again… or how I felt when I realized we'd both been shot, and that he'd saved my life. Whatever else happens in the future, I think I'd be hard-pressed to feel the way about anyone else - ever - the way I feel about Charlie.)

Anyway! I didn't mean to dwell so much on that part of the night. But it's kind of a big deal for me, since I've been married for so long and never expected to be having these types of conversations or feelings for another guy again.

After all that, and some more canoodling, another interesting conversation ensued.

It turns out, Charlie knows a few of the local cops pretty well. (Well, of course he does, it's a small town and he's one of the local favorites.) He poked and prodded a little bit about the investigation, and got a few details.

The police did, in fact, question the contractor guy I mentioned. He did have a red truck registered to him, and it did have a "Vermont Strong" license plate in 2012. But he claims the truck was stolen a few months ago. And that he never bothered to report it because it wasn't worth that much to begin with (and he didn't have insurance on it) so he just got on with his life.

The thing is, no-one's seen a new truck. No other vehicle is registered to his name. So if the red truck really did get stolen, what's he been driving? Why hasn't he bought something else?

When questioned, the neighbors don't remember seeing a different truck around the property. But no-one remembers the last time they saw the red truck, either. Could be last week - could be a few months ago. Entirely unhelpful.

The cops did poke around the property a little, and there was no sign of the red truck. Although he also has a dirt and gravel driveway, and the cops said it did look like something had driven on it fairly recently.

But aside from my suspicions, and the fact that the story about his red truck getting stolen didn't quite add up, the police really don't have any direct evidence. It's all circumstantial. Until they can find the truck and match it with the one in my surveillance video - or even better, match its tire tracks with my drive - they can't put him at my place. And he *claims* not to own a gun, although they don't have enough evidence to get a search warrant so they can't go through his house. If they could find the gun, they might be able to match it to the bullet that shot us. But it would have to be a rifle with a laser scope, and that's not the kind of thing that hides easily.

The cops did ask around at the local gun shops and sporting good stores, but they're all in larger cities, so it's unlikely the people there would know the contractor by name or on sight. So flashing his picture or asking if someone bought that kind of weapon there didn't really help. And who knows how recently he bought it, anyway? He could have had it for years - this is big hunting country - so the chance of finding records of him purchasing it - without a subpoena and a lot of digging - is pretty slim.

So... long story short, the investigation has hit a wall. The cops think there's a decent possibility that it's him, because they don't buy the story of the truck - but if it really was stolen, it could be pretty much anyone. And they have no way to prove anything, as long as he doesn't slip up and get seen driving the truck now.

It's great to finally have an update, and to know that the cops did some digging. But it sucks to know there's nothing else we can do, really - that I have to wait to be a victim again.

Or worse - that my son could be a victim next time.

Friday, June 12, 2015

Ugh. I drove back down to Boston yesterday, to spend the evening with Ben. It was so good to see him again… and so unpleasant to be in that house.

I packed up some more of my stuff. I've got my off-season clothes, now, and my coats and shoes that I haven't had room to take before. Maybe the next time I'm here, I'll grab some of my kitchen gadgets. Jim is decent in the kitchen, but he doesn't do any baking at all, so at the very least I could take that stuff. And I want my crock pot. And maybe my pressure cooker. And definitely my dutch oven, which my grandparents bought for us before they passed.

Gah, the business of dividing up 15 years of stuff is depressing as Hell.

And being here, where Jim very fervently doesn't want me, is bad for my psyche.

And being away from Charlie is hard right now. We're still trying to keep things casual and take things slow, but it's hard when he's at my place every night anyway. It would be very easy to fall into… something. But we haven't even been out on a date. We've just done a lot of work on my house together, and spent a lot of nights together - long, platonic nights. And a few not-so-platonic, now.

But when I'm in Boston, in that guest bedroom all alone, with Jim hating me on the other side of the hall… I really miss Charlie a lot then. Not the romantic stuff - just his solid, comforting presence.

It's mid-afternoon and I'm back in Vermont. Just went to the grocery to pick up some stuff for the weekend. Charlie will be here in a few hours, and I'm so looking forward to being with him.

Monday, June 15, 2015

I don't even know what to write. Where to start. The world feels… completely different. Shifted around me. Or maybe I've shifted, and the world is still the same as it's always been.

What can I even write?

Well…

I'm safe. Charlie is safe. And now, when Ben comes here, he'll be safe, too.

Friday, June 19, 2015

The police came out this week to ask a few questions. It seems that creepy contractor guy never reported to work on Monday, and someone reported him missing around the middle of the week.

The cops wanted to know if he'd been seen around here.

Or if the guy who had been making the nocturnal visits - and who shot Charlie and me - had been back.

Nothing to say, officers.

Wednesday, June 24, 2015

Rumors are flying around Island Pond right now.

Turns out, the red truck that never got reported stolen was recovered. It was parked along the side of the road on a stretch of empty highway.

The driver was nowhere to be found.

But they did find a rifle with a laser scope in a case behind the seat.

And a flashlight on the passenger's side floor.

There was a small radio with an earpiece attached, tuned to the police radio frequency, in the glove compartment.

Rumor says they swept it for prints, but never found anything besides the contractor guy's own fingerprints.

Charlie says they've filed away all the evidence in our shooting case, and they're ready to prosecute the guy if he ever turns up. His friends in the force said the ballistics test on the rifle came back as a match for the bullet that shot us, and the contractor's prints were all over the gun.

It's comforting to know the cops have everything ready to prosecute if the guy ever turns up.

Pity he's gone missing.

Friday, June 26, 2015

Ben's off to camp this morning. I rode with Jim to drop him off, because I didn't want to miss it and I'd be damned if I was going to let a pissy soon-to-be-ex-husband keep me from enjoying something that my boy was so excited about. Or keep me away from my last chance to see the kid before he's gone for an entire month at camp.

The drive out to Western Mass wasn't quite as awkward as I was expecting. I guess the passing of a little time has started to ease the anger.

Honestly, I feel like a different person versus who I was when all of this started. So much has happened in the past six months. I've been through so much - and grown so much - that I just don't even know how to relate to Jim anymore. My concerns are so different from his.

Really, I feel a little sad for him. He's stuck in this work-a-day world, going to an office and coming home again every day. He's not doing anything to prepare for the future, and he's really not even living his life right now.

The world is so fragile. Everything could come crashing down in an instant. Human life gets snuffed out like a candle in the blink of an eye - every single day. And he's living a life completely oblivious to this reality, without any attempt to protect himself or his family, or to prepare for a time when the world changes.

And here I am at the opposite extreme now. I've bought a house in the middle of nowhere, with enough land to grow food and off-the-grid systems to ensure we can maintain the comforts of home long after the electrical grid goes down, or the satellite systems go dark, or the economy collapses, or rising gas prices fuel a national panic that leads to rioting and the collapse of our civilization. Whatever happens, I'm ready for it.

ISIS? No problem. Ebola? Not an issue. Russia triggers World War III? Nothing for us to worry about. A massive hurricane wipes out the East Coast? My family is safe.

The *only* thing I'm not prepared for is nuclear winter, and that's intentional. If that happens, I don't want to sit around in a bunker and watch the world die around me, knowing I'm one of a handful of humans who have survived and waiting quietly for my species to go extinct. In that case, I want to go quickly. If the first blast doesn't take us out, I've got what I need to ease us quietly and peacefully into oblivion before radiation sickness sets in.

So Jim can plod miserably through his meaningless, unprepared life, waiting with all the other cattle for a slaughter he doesn't believe is coming.

I - I've been tested, and I know the lengths I'll go to in order to keep my family safe. I'll carry on with my stockpiling, and work on learning new skills for self-sufficiency, so that when the worst happens, Charlie and Ben and I can lead a happy, plentiful life, unaffected by whatever disaster reduces our population to a fraction of what it is today.

Because make no mistake, it is coming. You can smell it on the wind. See it in the news headlines. We humans are a burden that has grown too heavy for our world. The reaping will come soon enough, and when it does… only the prepared will survive.

THE END